DARKNESS IS MY SHADOW

DARKNESS IS MY SHADOW

BY

VICTOR C. BROWN, JR.
AND
JOAN L. BROWN

ISBN # 1-58721-950-6

1stbooks rev.- 5/9/00

DEDICATIONS

"It takes a woman to raise a woman." My mother is quite a woman. Her influence, love, and support have given me an understanding of human nature. She's always there when her family or friends need her. But she will let you know when she disagrees with you. She keeps each of us on track, especially her husband of forty-seven years. She may have to repeat herself to Dad, but it amazes me how he can hear the rest of us without his hearing aid. Thank you, Mom, for all you've given me. Life has been hard, but it has had its rewards.

Another great lady who has left her mark is my aunt, Sr. Richard. She asks for so little from the world and has devoted her life to the service of others. Her example and dedication have left their imprint on me.

To the two women who have influenced my life, I dedicate this book so others may know that happiness can be found even in darkness.

JS

In the world today, people come down on their doctors and the medical field because they feel these professionals are driven only by the making of big bucks. In this story, you'll meet Dr. King. Even though this story is fiction, the doctor is real. When I first met him, I was a beat-up old coach. My body had so many aches and pains, it was hard to walk. The headaches from previous injuries made my days unbearable. Despite the pain and injury, I was still coaching a hockey team. Dr. King thought this unwise, but he didn't take away my last enjoyment in life. He put in long hours trying to put my body back into some kind of shape as well as my soul. He never worried about monetary payment, even though I did. He was not just my doctor, he turned into my friend. There may be other doctors like Dr. King As the co-author of this story, I feel that not only the LaBuld family has its star, I also have my own star within my Dr. King.

VCB

CHAPTER ONE

The sun was rising as the patients were waking into another day of resentment. Some didn't care if this day came or not. William LaBuld was one of those people. He had been brought to the hospital a week ago from Vietnam. He had lost the sight in both his eyes as well as his will to live. He had been the greatest prospective hockey player that the town of Ogdensburg, New York, had to offer. But now all he cared to remember was that the ice was just as cold as the void within his heart. He'd never see the inside of another ice arena again. His thoughts were, "Why was I drafted? Why did I have to lose my eyes? What did I do that was so bad that God punished me this way? I went to church every week and honored my Father and Mother and obeyed the rest of the Commandments. Why me?"

As he stared at the wall without knowing the color of it, a nurse came into his room. Her name was Katherine Toia. With a cheerful smile on her face she said, "Good morning, William."

William replied, "What's so damn good about it? I can't see it."

"Well," she answered, "for one thing, I have some pills for you to take that will make you feel better. Your breakfast will be here soon. The best thing is that your Mother is coming to see you."

"Can you give me new eyes?" he asked her sarcastically.

"Now look, William, if you're looking for pity you'll get none from me."

Miss Kay, as her patients called her, had seen some of the worst cases, mostly young men returning from Vietnam. Anything William said to her wouldn't shock her in the slightest. She knew the best approach was not to pity these men: pity would only make them weak. Sometimes, the patients thought the words coming from her mouth were cruel, but little did they know that her heart was crying out to them, but she had to be strong.

"There are a lot of men in here just as badly off as you are. They saw action just as you did," added Miss Kay. "At least

1

they get their butts out of bed and try to help themselves. They're not whining all day and feeling sorry for themselves."

"Why you bitch! If the shoe were on the other foot, I'd like to see what the hell you would do."

"Well, the shoe isn't on the other foot, and you are not my only patient. So let me earn my money and get you dressed into some clean pajamas before you tell everybody I'm not doing my job."

William was shocked at her reply and didn't say a word after that.

As noon drew near, Miss Kay came into his room with a wheelchair and took him to the recreation room where his mother was waiting. As she bent down and hugged her son, the tears from Ada LaBuld's eyes wet her son's robe. It was hard to tell if William was crying - his eyes were still covered with bandages. "Oh, son," she cried, "I've missed you so much."

William had lost his father two years before he had gone into the service. All he had now was his mother and a girl back home. One of the first questions he asked his mother was how she was. Elizabeth Smith and William were to be married as soon as he was discharged.

"Does Elizabeth know I am blind, Mother?"

Ada replied, "Everybody in Ogdensburg knows."

"Oh God."

"It's nothing to feel ashamed about. Everyone is so proud of you."

"I didn't ask you that. I don't care about everybody else. What does Elizabeth think?" asked William.

His mother responded, "She says that she can't wait to see you."

"That's a lot of bull shit. If she wanted to see me she would have come with you."

"She must have written you that she was teaching figure skating to children."

"You mean to tell me she couldn't have taken off to come up here to Buffalo with you?"

Ada didn't know how to answer him so she quickly started talking about all the things the town of Ogdensburg was going to

2

give him: a big home-coming party when he was well enough to leave the Veterans Hospital in Buffalo.

When William heard this, he exclaimed in anguish, "A coming-home party. Wow, that's the greatest thing I have to look forward to? Mom, you don't understand. I'll never skate or play hockey again. I can't even make a living. I don't want to learn to make wallets or string beads."

"But you'll get a nice pension from the service."

"Big deal! A pension from the service. Don't you realize that I had a chance to play for Montreal before I got drafted? I had the world right in my hands. Now, I can't even see it," William responded bitterly. "I had a girl who wrote me letters in Vietnam and told me she loved me. We'd be married as soon as I got out. Now I don't even know about that."

With a heavy heart, Ada consoled her son. "Well, you have me, William. I will take care of you. Besides, I never did like you playing hockey. It's such a violent sport. You could have gotten hurt there, too."

"Violent," William retorted, "you don't know what violence is until you go to war, and no one cheers you there."

Suddenly, there was a commotion: in the ward for the hard-core, severely disturbed, a patient was screaming, "I don't want to go home. I want to go back to Nam. My friends are waiting there for me."

Nurses rushed to the disturbance and put the man in restraints as Ada watched with anxiety. A hospital is a place to help heal, but it is also a place where mothers have to witness suffering and pain. Mothers remembered their joy of bringing new life into the world now experienced that life having been destroyed and needing to be rebuilt.

A nurse and the doctor who had just treated the raving patient were standing next to William and his mother. "This is good," commented the doctor. "We might have sent him back into the world."

"But, doctor, he seemed ready to go home."

"You just can't trust those Special Forces. They think differently. This country made a machine and doesn't know how to disassemble it. They think we doctors are miracle workers. My heart bleeds for their families."

As William and his mother listened, Ada remarked, "See, William, war has struck a lot of people in different ways. We mothers have to thank God that our sons are still alive."

"Alive! When I played hockey, people came to the games. They cheered. Are people going to cheer because I am blind? No, I can't accept that. I don't know what I'm going to do yet, but I do know I'm not going back to Ogdensburg. I have nothing now."

Ada was in tears, she wanted to cry, but she knew it would upset her son. The doctors had told her what a terrible ordeal he had been through while in the hospital in Vietnam and that it might be even more traumatic for him when he returned to the States. She was told to be calm and strong and to go along with whatever William said to her. He was under a great mental strain.

William and his mother talked a while longer. Miss Kay came into the room and said, "Well, Mrs. LaBuld, I think I'm going to have to take your handsome son upstairs for his dinner now."

Ada looked at her son, then hugged him and kissed the bandages over his eyes. "I'll be back in a few days. It was quite a trip from Ogdensburg to Buffalo. The weather is getting bad now. These late autumn days can be treacherous. Before you know it, Thanksgiving will be here."

Miss Kay pushed William back to his room where his tray of food awaited for him. She gently removed his robe and helped him into the bed where she began to feed him. "Well, William, tomorrow should be an eventful day for you. I see by your chart that you're going to start school."

William pushed away the spoon from her hand and angrily said, "What school?"

"They are going to teach you how to walk by yourself with the use of a cane."

"Are they going to give me a tin cup, too?"

"I've seen many men come back from the war a lot worse off than you. They managed to find a place in this world where they

4

were useful. They didn't go and hide in some corner. Life is still beautiful, William. There are many things you can still do."

"Will I be able to get married? Do you know a girl who wants a blind nothing for a husband?"

"Someone who loves you won't let that stand in her way. In fact, if I were twenty years younger, I'd be interested in you myself. But if you could see my face, it would probably stop your wrist watch. Do you remember the Frankenstein movies? I tried out for the bride of Frankenstein, but they told me I was too ugly for the part."

That made William smile. In fact, that was the first time Miss Kay had seen him smile in the week that he'd been there.

"You know, William, it's only 1967, that makes you about twenty-one years old, right?"

"How do you know how old I am?"

"Well, I go through all my patients' records to see if I can find an eligible bachelor."

William smiled and said, "You're not that ugly, are you?"

"Would it matter if I was, William? You know, even people with good eyes are blind sometimes. Beauty is in the heart. Think about that for a while, William."

She patted him on the knee and said in a soft tone of voice, "Well, William, I have other patients I must take care of now. I'll be back to get you in the morning. Have a good night."

That evening, the chaplain visited William. "Are you William LaBuld?" the priest inquired.

William, enveloped in darkness, responded, "I'm William LaBuld."

"My name is Father Vonesh. Your mother has asked me to stop in to talk to you."

"I need nothing from you. Nor do I need anything from God. I just want to be left alone."

The priest understood William's anger. He knew William needed more time to adjust to the loss of his sight. Father Vonesh replied, "I'm here when you need me, William. You'll be in my prayers."

"I don't need your prayers or your pity!"

5

Father Vonesh did not want to upset William so he said good night and left.

The next morning, as Miss Kay was feeding William his breakfast, she revealed a little more about herself and her past. William seemed to appreciate her a bit more. He began talking about his childhood and how he loved hockey so much when he was growing up. It was good therapy for him to talk about his life before the war.

"You know, William, there's another hockey player in the hospital."

William's interest was aroused. "What's his name?"

"Victor Wolf."

"Did he also lose his eyes?"

"No, he lost more than his eyes."

"If he lost more than his eyes, he's got to be dead."

Quietly, she sighed, "He lost his soul, along with a few others."

"I'd like to meet this Victor Wolf."

"I'm sorry, William. He's on a special ward in the hospital. He's not allowed any visitors without his doctor's permission."

Finally Miss Kay said, "Well, William, let's get you into your wheelchair and go for a ride."

"Where are you going to take me?"

"We're going to school today. Don't you remember?"

"Can't we skip it for a couple more days?"

"I don't think so. Let's not put off for tomorrow what we can do today."

William grumbled a bit, but Miss Kay managed to talk him into going. She helped him into his wheelchair and they rode down the elevator. When the doors opened, they heard men talking and laughing. William wondered what was going on.

Miss Kay hadn't wheeled him far when she approached the doctor. "Good morning, Major Fisher. I've brought you a new patient. This is William LaBuld."

The major shook William's hand. "Nice to meet you. You'll be spending a great deal of time here in therapy. I'm sure you'll be making some friends. Miss Kay will be back for you later."

He wheeled William over to another patient who was in a wheelchair. As he did, William heard someone say, "Hi, there. My name is Ed Brunetti. I'm one of the mice in this place. What's your name?"

"William."

"Army, Navy, or Marines?"

"Army."

"Well, I'm a leatherneck myself. This must be your first time down here. As soon as we're done with our exercises, I'll introduce you to the rest of the mice."

"The mice," William asked curiously, "what do you mean?"

Then Ed started laughing. "Haven't you heard of the Three Blind Mice?"

William didn't know how to take his guy: he was blind, too, but why was he joking about it? He didn't know it at the time, but in a few weeks William would be joking also, and it would be Ed who would change his attitude towards Life.

In those next few weeks, William found out that Ed had a wife and two children, and they were sticking by him all the way. He also discovered that one of Ed's high school girlfriends was one of the nurses - Lorraine Olson. Although Lorraine and Ed had long since buried any romantic involvement, there was still a sensitive compassion, of which Ed took advantage. Lorraine had enjoyed being Ed's girl in high school, now she was proud to be one of the people who appreciated his service to his country.

William found the exercises were tough. Many times, he tripped and fell on his face, smashed into walls, and opened wrong doors. But he kept on trying. Being an athlete helped him a great deal, he had good coordination. Before long, everyone noticed his attitude changed. William was becoming a perfectionist at his therapy. His mother and his girlfriend, Elizabeth, were visiting him twice a week, too. Things were looking up. Major Fisher had told him it would be a matter of a few weeks and he'd be able to return home and start getting his life back together.

Deep down inside, William knew that life for him would never be the same. One day, as he was walking with his cane through the hospital, he was testing himself. He was trying to use the elevator - with the loss of his eyesight it was no longer a simple, commonplace act to push an elevator button. It became a major obstacle. Once on the elevator, William became aware of two fellow passengers. He overheard their conversation. One veteran was commenting that he couldn't go home when he was released, he was appealing to his friend to procure a gun for him. The other vet tried to quiet his friend by agreeing that he didn't want to go home either. The desperate vet told him not to worry, the other passenger was only a blind man.

When the elevator stopped, William followed the two passengers. A nurse quickly approached him and told him that this was not his floor - it was a floor for the loony tunes.

Outraged, William quickly responded, "Nurse, this is a military hospital. These men have given themselves to their country. You have no right to call them loony tunes!"

The embarrassed nurse's face reddened as she realized how true William's statement was. She apologized as she helped him onto the elevator. As he rode down to his floor he thought, "If an educated, compassionate nurse thinks this way about the patients she's committed to helping, what must the rest of the world think when they see a blind man?"

William felt despondent until he walked into therapy. Being with Ed bolstered his spirits. Ed was commenting on the good-looking therapist. As she was lecturing to the patients, Ed asked her why she was wearing blue panties today.

The bewildered therapist was flustered to be asked about the color of her panties: he was right - they were blue!

Ed made another statement regarding her black bra: the colors just didn't match.

The stunned therapist wondered if Ed was really blind. Because she was working with the blind, she thought she didn't have to worry about sitting like a lady or what she wore. Now she wondered how many faux pas he had seen.

As Ed was asking these questions, the other patients kept asking what colors were her underwear. The student nurses were blushing and burst out laughing with the patients.

8

The therapist realized from reading Ed's chart that he was totally blind. Could it be a million in one shot that he correctly guessed the color of her underwear? She didn't know that she had been set up by Ed. Lorraine had been Ed's stool pigeon. She had seen the therapist changing in the locker room and obediently reported the woman's underwear colors as Ed had once asked her to do. Lorraine didn't know the reason for the strange request until she heard through the grapevine of the miracle cure of a blind man in the therapy room. One thing the therapist did know was that Ed was giving everyone a sense of humor and that made her work a little easier. William himself was assimilating this sense of humor and laughter.

A couple days later in therapy, William never said a word. The scuttlebutt around the hospital was that one of the Special Forces had blown off his head. The doctors were mystified as to where he could have gotten the gun, but William could never forget the elevator conversation and the desperation in the voices he'd overheard.

As he was once again navigating the hospital with his cane, William eavesdropped on a conversation between student nurses: how they were afraid to go up to the severely mentally disturbed ward, and how one of those soldiers, Victor Wolf, was so handsome but had the scariest eyes. William recalled hearing that name from Miss Kay. In the back of his mind, he wondered if God had it in for hockey players.

A few days later Frank Gore, a long-time hockey playing friend from Ogdensburg, arrived to visit William. They talked for a couple of hours about old times. Out of the blue, Frank asked, "Remember your old girlfriend Elizabeth? Looks like her and that fag are going to get married."

"What do you mean?"

"You remember that Richard Saunders, don't you? That kid that used to figure skate with the girls when all of us other guys were playing hockey. Well, he and Elizabeth have been teaching figure skating together to the kids for the past year or so. I guess they're planning on getting married soon."

"That's nice. I hope they're happy."

William didn't say anything more for a while and then politely told Frank he was getting a little tired and wanted to rest. Using his cane, he walked Frank to the elevator, pushed the button for his friend, and waited with emptiness in his heart.

Alone in his room, William laid in bed, thinking about how he was trying to become a whole man again, and now this. For hours, he tried to piece the puzzle together. Elizabeth had been coming to visit him under false pretenses. Apparently she had been going with Richard even when his eyes were still good. But why did his mother lie to him? Why didn't anyone tell him? Then he thought about his friend Ed who was working hard in school because he was planning on doing something when he got back into society. Most importantly, Ed had the support and loyalty of his wife and kids. As William closed his eyes, he kept repeating over and over to himself, "I am going to show those people. I'll show them all. I don't need anyone."

In therapy the next day, William and Ed discussed their plans when they were released from the hospital. Ed told William he was going to Chicago.

"Chicago, what's there?"

"Well, they have a great school for the blind."

"What's the name of it?"

"Lighthouse for the Blind."

"What's so great about it?"

"According to Dr. Fisher, I'll be able to learn to read Braille and get vocational training, too. My blindness is not going to stop me. I have a lot to live for. Besides that, my sister lives there and she's got a house she's going to give me."

"Sounds to me like you've got a hell of a sister."

"She's alright. Hey listen, she's got money. And moreover, her old man thinks I'm some kind of a hero. When they give me the house, my sister's husband will tell his friends and that will make him look like a hero, too. You see, he was one of those '4-F'ers.' He'll feel like he did something during the war, even though he couldn't serve. What are you going to do when you leave here, William?"

"Go play hockey and maybe be a referee. You know most of them are blinder than we are. Seriously though, I don't really know. I do know I am going to get away from this area to some place where nobody knows me."

"Really? What about your mother and your girl?"

"I have my mother and that's about all."

Ed got the picture. "Hey, listen, I've got a great idea. Why don't you come to Chicago with me?"

William wanted to say yes, but he knew Ed had a family to worry about. It would be hard enough on his wife to take care of one blind person, let alone two. "I'd like to, but I can't. Thanks, anyway."

"Why not? We could go to school together. You'd be doing me a favor."

"A favor?"

"Yeah, I've got problems, too. I've got my kids and I don't really know how they are going to react with me being blind. I was thinking that if they saw both of us together, they might not think of me as being a freak. If my friend the hockey player were there, they'd realize that being blind could happen to anyone."

"That's a lot of bull shit. Nothing seems to bother you."

"You're wrong, William. It bothers me so much that I don't want my kids to ever see me like this."

William knew the hurt Ed was feeling, just like when he thought about hockey and how he'd never see the people up in the bleachers or skate with the puck again.

"What do you think your wife would say about me coming with you?"

"Well, I talked with her last week. I told her I wasn't sure if I was coming home, but if you came with you could change all of that. I'm sure my wife would feel the same way, especially if she knew it would help me."

"How about letting me think it over, Ed."

For the last time in the hospital, William would hear the name Victor Wolf: the doctors and nurses were complaining about military justice. It seemed that now that they had gotten Victor Wolf well, he was headed for a court martial. Some of the doctors anticipated he'd spend the rest of his life in jail.

11

William could not understand how a man could be wounded from a military act and be sent to prison.

William was thinking about Ed's proposition and didn't make his decision until his mother and Elizabeth came to see him. Immediately he said to Elizabeth, "I hear you're engaged."

Elizabeth was stunned. It was so quiet in the room, you could hear a pin drop.

"Why did you have to lie about it?" William continued. "Did you think you were going to break my heart? I really feel lucky I found out. God only took my eyes, you would have taken my self-respect."

Elizabeth snapped right back at him. "I came up here because I didn't want the people in Ogdensburg to think I didn't have a heart. I was trying to be nice to you. Right now they're talking behind my back."

Ada disagreed, "That's not true, Elizabeth."

"Don't tell me what's true. I thought I could tell your son in a nice way and he could give me the same courtesy back by understanding."

Confronting William, Elizabeth burst out, "Why couldn't you have gone to college. Then they wouldn't have drafted you. You would have been just a hockey player: a man with stitches in his face who can only brag in bars. It wasn't meant to be from the beginning, William."

"Then why did we make plans to get married?"

Elizabeth was shrouded in silence. William persisted, "I'll tell you why. Because I was a star. It made your prestige around town a little greater."

Ada sat as though she were going to have a stroke. She didn't know what to say to her son or Elizabeth.

Anger inflamed William. "The only understanding I need to give you is my pity. I can see why people are talking behind your back. They're probably wondering which one is going to be the bride." With that remark, Elizabeth stormed out the door.

"And you, Mother. How could you come up here and lie to me, too? I guess I'll never know the answer. Did anybody ever stop to think of when I got out of here? I've been made the fool by both of you."

12

"I didn't say anything to you because I didn't want to upset you."

"All I can say, Mother, is that you and everybody else had no right to make my decision for me. If Ed and his wife want me, I'm going to Chicago and live with them for a while."

"What are you talking about, William. Your home is Ogdensburg. I will take care of you. I'm your mother."

"But mothers are supposed to tell their sons the truth."

"You can't mean that, William. What about the friends and everyone waiting for you back in Ogdensburg?"

"I could care less."

"Oh, William," Ada said with tears in her eyes. "You can't go and live with strangers. You wouldn't feel right. I've been waiting for you to come home for so long."

"The only reason you want me home with you is so you can tell all your friends how you're taking care of your little blind boy. I don't need that, Mother."

Ada began crying. "That's not fair. That's not the reason at all."

William mellowed a bit. "Look, Mom, they have a good school in Chicago that my friend Ed was telling me about. I'll be able to learn to read Braille there. I'll be getting a nice pension from the service. I'll be able to devote a lot of time to learning. I might as well take advantage of it. If you want to, you can come and visit me once in a while. Don't you see, I've got to try it on my own. I don't want to be where people will pity me. This is something I must do."

Ada shook her head as the tears continued. She tried for the next ten minutes to convince William out of going to Chicago. But she saw his mind was made up. She realized he had to have a sense of independence and purpose. Perhaps going to Chicago would help him adjust to his new way of life. She hoped that eventually he'd come back to his home in Ogdensburg.

After Ada left, William rang for the nurse to take him to Ed's room. As Miss Kay wheeled him into Ed's room, William asked, "Ed, are you here?"

Ed laughed. "Can't you see me, you dummy?"

13

They all smiled. Before William could speak, Ed demanded, "Well, what about it? Are you coming to Chicago with me?"

"What about your wife? What does she think?"

"She says you have a home as long as you want. She agrees with me that there would be less pressures if I had someone else around who knew what it was like to be in the same predicament."

"Then, it's settled. But if I'm imposing or get in the way, you promise me you'll let me know. Just think, when you and I go to school and learn how to read Braille, maybe we'll turn out to be a couple of gamblers."

"Gamblers?"

"Yeah. I've got it all figured out. We could mark the deck of cards with our little hole punches and set up our own games." Everyone laughed. "After all, who would shoot a blind man for cheating?"

"Seriously though, it looks like my wife will be here next Thursday for us. Be sure you get everything squared away. Before you know it, we'll be in the big city."

"Okay. Well, look, I'm kind of tired. I think I'll be going back to my room now. I've got a lot of thinking to do."

"Okay. I'll see you tomorrow."

As William and Miss Kay were going down the hall, she said, "It sounds like you're going to live with Ed and his wife in Chicago."

"Yeah, Miss Kay. I'm taking your advice. I'm not going to give up. I'm going to go to school out there with Ed."

"That's wonderful. Always keep in mind that life can be beautiful. You don't need eyes to see it."

"I don't know about that. But I can tell you that the best friend I ever had I found here in the hospital."

"You mean Ed?"

"I certainly do. I can remember when I was playing hockey, I was everybody's friend, their idol. I haven't seen many of my so-called friends coming here to visit me. You were right about one thing you told me a while ago: it's not what you see with your eyes, it's what you feel in your heart."

14

"It sounds to me that you've been doing some wise thinking lately, but I think it's time you rested, now."

Thursday came quickly.   William's mother was at the hospital and was introduced to Ed and his wife, June. William and Ed thanked the doctors, nurses, and of course Miss Kay for all the help and encouragement she had given them.   June had a cab waiting to take them to the train station.   Ada made one last attempt at the station to coax him into returning to Ogdensburg, but William's mind was made up.   She realized it was a useless attempt.   William kissed Ada goodbye and told her he would call her from time to time.   June reassured her that she'd take good care of him.   She whispered to Ada, "I'm not really stealing your son.   I've come to the conclusion that these two men need one another.   They can give each other a support we can't."

By that statement, Ada realized June was right.   Her selfishness in wanting her son would not stand in the way of his happiness.

CHAPTER TWO

On the trip to Chicago, William became better acquainted with June. She was too shy to tell him what a big help he'd been: William was Ed's comfort-zone. William continually asked, "Are you sure I'm not going to be a burden to you?"

When the train pulled into the station on Friday, Ed's sister, Connie, and her husband Mel were waiting with June and Ed's two children. The children were excited, they greeted Ed as though he were a king. They were polite as they were introduced to William. It was a touching scene when the boys grabbed onto their dad's legs and hugged him as they told him how much they missed him, even though they hardly knew him because of the war.

As Mel drove everyone to Ed's new home, they talked about Ed's younger years. Mel asked William a few questions about his home and his service action, but nothing was mentioned about the blindness of either William or Ed.

When they pulled up to the house, Mel asked, "You guys wouldn't mind, would you, if I have a few friends over here someday to meet you. I've told them I'd like to show them a couple of real heroes. After all, you guys did lose your eyes."

Connie whispered as she shook her head in disgust, "Oh, shut up. What are you saying?"

"That's alright," Ed broke the tension. "You bring anybody over that you want. Besides I can't thank you enough for the house and everything. Listen, my buddy, William is the hero, not me. Did you know he had a chance to play hockey for Montreal?"

"You didn't tell me that," said Mel.

"Well, it doesn't make any difference now," answered William. "Those days are gone forever. I don't think about them anymore."

Ed Jr. excitedly blurted out, "Wow, a hockey player. What position did you play?"

"I was a center."

17

"I play defense with the Mites over at Rainbo Arena. But next year, I'm going to be nine and then I'll be on a Squirt team. My brother Tommy is a center, too, just like you were. But he's still in the clinic. We're both going to be hockey players."

William smiled and said to Ed, "You didn't tell me your boys played hockey."

"Well, I didn't know if you were going to come and stay with us. So I figured I'd save it for a surprise. My wife had written me when I was in Nam. I wasn't sure if they were going to stick with it or not. It's such a rough sport for these little guys."

"That's only your impression, as well as a lot of others. Actually they wear good protective clothing. It looks a lot rougher than it is. If your sons have guts like their dad, they'll make really great hockey players."

Ed glowed at William's comments. Mel was sitting, listening to the conversation when June and Connie entered the room. Connie suggested that it was time they were leaving.

Afterwards, June escorted Ed and William through the house so they could get acquainted with their new surroundings. The last room June showed them was William's. She guided them around it so they would know where the bed, dresser, and closet were located. June had gone for a couple of days to the Lighthouse for the Blind and discovered that it would be best if she removed excessive furniture so the rooms wouldn't be cluttered and present an obstacle course. The boys also understood that they couldn't leave their toys laying about where they would cause an accident.

"I hope this is alright, William," June commented.

"Oh, I'm sure it will be just fine. By the way, we haven't had a chance to talk about money. I'd like you and Ed to have half of my pension check each month."

"We'll talk about that some other time. It's wonderful having you here with us."

"Why don't we have some coffee?" asked Ed.

"I'm a little tired, Ed. I'd like to get some rest, if you don't mind." William sensed that Ed and his family would like to be alone, so he excused himself and asked June to shut the door so he could get ready for bed.

"Can you make it alright?" asked June. "Now don't be bashful. My husband isn't a jealous man."

William blushed. "I can make it alright, June. Thank you, anyway."

For the next few weeks, William enjoyed being around Ed and his family. The boys told William about their hockey experiences. William was in a good mood, for it seemed that hockey was still a part of his life.

Each morning, June drove Ed and William to the Lighthouse for the Blind. The people there were wonderful. Ed, of course, evolved into the class clown. This optimist bolstered everyone, he made it fun going to school.

One survival skill they mastered was commuting by bus. After class, they had to cross a few streets and board the Ashland bus for the northward trek from Wood and Roosevelt to Ashland and Irving Park, about a block away from their house. It took them a couple months to learn the system.

Another skill they perfected was reading Braille. William was aggravated because there were so few books about sports. He was adjusting to his new life in Chicago, although he kept in close contact with his mother.

Usually on their bus ride home, William and Ed didn't sit next to each other because the school felt they'd gain more expertise by traveling independently. Ed usually found a passenger with whom he'd shoot the breeze, while William sat quietly by himself. The friends continued to gain confidence in their ability to navigate the city.

One evening following their usual routine, William and Ed boarded the bus: Ed wandered off to find a kibitzer while William found himself a seat next to a window. The next bus stop brought a passenger who sat next to William and asked, "It was a nice day out today, wasn't it?"

William didn't reply. Instead he thought, "Isn't it funny how people never talk to strangers, but they somehow like to talk to blind people. I guess they must feel safe. After all, blind people never hurt anyone."

William heard Ed's voice every once in a while. The woman next to him didn't say any more until they got to Ashland and Irving Park.

Since William and Ed regularly took this bus, the driver knew to call out their stop. As William stood up and grabbed his cane, he heard the woman address him. "Pardon me, but I believe you're taking my cane."

"I'm sorry, madam, but this is my cane."

The woman put her hand on the cane. "Sir, this is my cane. If you'll look at it, you'll see it's for a blind person."

"That's right, madam. It's for me. I am the blind person."

The woman thought William was mocking her. "You must have no respect for anyone, you jerk."

Her voice was loud enough for the bus driver to get up from his seat, walk down toward them, and ask what the trouble was.

The woman explained, "This man won't give me my cane."

William answered, "This is my cane and she's trying to take it."

The bus driver looked towards the window and saw William's cane. "Here, put your hand by the window. Your cane is there."

William retrieved his cane and quickly apologized. "I'm sorry. You see, I'm blind and I thought this was my cane and you were trying to take it."

The woman laughed. "Well, can't you see, I'm blind, too."

"How can I, if I'm blind?" They both laughed.

The woman continued, "I don't believe this. I thought you were one of those smart kids trying to give me a hard time. Are you really blind, too?"

"I certainly am."

They were both still laughing when the bus driver interrupted them. "I hate to break this up, but we're holding up traffic."

The woman and William got off the bus. William called, "Ed, are you here?"

"I'm here," said Ed, laughing. "I was just enjoying your little predicament."

"Well, come over here. I'd like you to meet - to meet, you know, I don't even know your name."

"It's Mary Cannon."

"My name's William LaBuld. This is my friend, Ed Brunetti."

Ed was still laughing. William asked, "What's so funny, Ed?"

"Look at us. We're like the three blind mice standing on a corner. The people passing by must think we're a little off. Well, I can't stand here and laugh all night. I'll meet you back at the house." Ed found someone to help him across the street.

When Ed arrived home, June asked him where William was.

"Some hooker picked him up on the bus. And to top it off, she's blind, too."

"Oh Ed, be serious. Where is he?"

"He's by the bus stop talking to this woman. He'll be alright."

About half an hour later, William walked through the door. "I'm sorry I'm late for dinner, June. I met someone on the bus and we started talking after we got off."

Ed popped up and said, "Did you score? Oh, I guess not. You didn't have enough time."

"You know, Ed, sometimes you're not so funny," said June. "Who is she, William?"

"All I know so far is that she lives two blocks west of Ashland on Irving Park. That's around here somewhere. But you'll never believe how we met." He related the episode.

June though it was funny, too.

William told them he was going to have lunch with her at a restaurant at Polk and Paulina. Ed knew where it was - right around the corner from Cook County Hospital where Mary Cannon worked.

"You mean to tell me, you're going on a blind date?"

"You know, Ed, it really is a blind date." And they all laughed.

That night, as William laid in bed thinking about Mary, he wondered what she looked like and how she had become blind.

21

He also thought about Elizabeth back in Ogdensburg, until he finally dropped off to sleep.

The next day in school, William couldn't concentrate. His thoughts centered on Mary and their luncheon date. He could hardly wait until noon. William had to tell his teachers that he was going out to lunch and that he would be alright alone, and that he would be back for his afternoon classes.

Everyone had been teasing him all morning because Ed kept chanting, "William's got a girlfriend."

Finally noon approached. William walked out of school, tapping his cane along the sidewalk. He remembered Miss Kay's advice: he could love just like any normal man, after all, love was something you didn't have to see to experience.

When William reached the rendezvous at the mailbox on the corner of Polk and Paulina in front of the restaurant, he leaned against it to wait for Mary. It seemed as though he had waited for an eternity when someone touched his hand and asked, "Can I help you, sir?"

It was only a bystander trying to help.

William was feeling disappointed and thought to himself, "Did she change her mind?"

Finally he heard a voice, "Are you here, William?"

"Mary, is that you?"

"It's me."

William's spirits soared.

"I'm sorry I'm late. I was afraid you wouldn't wait. I had an emergency at the hospital and I had to do some x-rays."

"Oh, that's alright. X-rays?"

"Right. That's what I do for my living, William."

William thought to himself, "How could she take x-rays?"

William and Mary walked into the crowded restaurant. There weren't any open tables. Two nurses had just sat down and offered them their table. Ordinarily, William wouldn't have accepted their offer; but this was different, he was with a girl now. He thanked them. They sat down and ordered their lunch.

While eating, they talked about everything they hadn't spoken about the night before. Mary was impressed that he had been a hockey player. He was just as impressed that she was an

22

x-ray technician at the hospital. She had been born blind and had gone to school a long time to train for the job. In fact, there had been magazine articles written about her because it was so unusual for a blind person to be in that line of work. Mary inquired if he had any girlfriends. William told her that he had one once, but not any more.

Finally Mary said, "Well, William, I've really enjoyed this, but I think it's time I get back to the hospital."

"How do you know what time it is?"

"I have a Braille watch. Haven't they taught you yet in school?"

"Not yet. Maybe you could teach me how. I'll get a watch like yours."

Although William couldn't see her smiling, Mary replied, "I'll be glad to, William."

As they left the restaurant, William told Mary he would like to walk her back to work, but he was afraid he might get lost. They agreed to meet each other at the bus stop that night and go home together on the bus.

For several months, William and Mary established a routine: they rode the bus together in the morning, had lunch at the restaurant, and at the end of the day rode home until they separated to go their own ways. Ed and June were happy that William had a lady friend, although they were concerned about how quiet he was. The only real conversations he had were about hockey with Ed's children.

One evening, on the bus trip home, William asked Mary, "Do you ever have company over to your house?"

"I haven't had anyone over since my father died. My mother died when I was still a little child and my father raised me. I hardly saw him. He drank a lot. He would get someone to watch me when I was younger, but as I got older, I always seemed to be alone. That's why I went to school to become a technician. In the hospital I'm always around people. Even though I cant's see them, I feel I belong somewhere. But my nights are lonely, William. I do think about you a lot."

"Do you really mean that?"

"Yes, I do."

"My nights are lonely, too."

"Do you realize that we don't even know what the other looks like?"

"It's not what a person looks like. It's what they feel in their heart." William was surprised to hear himself uttering Miss Kay's words.

"You know, William, I never want to wait until the next day to meet you. It always seems so long in between."

Then William said in a choked voice, "I feel the same way, Mary. I wish we could be together all the time. The only other time I've felt this much happiness was when I was skating."

"That sounds like a proposal to me. Is it?"

"That wouldn't be a bad idea. I'm not joking. I know we've known each other less than a year, but you bring me such happiness."

"I hope I give you happiness. I know you do for me."

They were both silent, until Mary said, "I've got a great idea. Why don't you come and live with me. In that way, both of us can tell how it will work out."

"Do you really mean that?"

"I wouldn't have asked you if I didn't mean it."

"Look, why don't you come home with Ed and me tonight and have dinner with us?"

Just then the bus was pulling up to their stop. All three got off. William couldn't wait to tell Ed the good news. He asked Ed to go home ahead of him and tell June he was bringing Mary home with him for dinner.

Mary was as excited as Ed. In fact, Ed couldn't wait to get home and tell June.

"Are you sure it's alright with your friend's wife?"

"Of course."

"I feel so embarrassed, and a little afraid. How will I get home?"

"Ed's wife June will drive you home. And please don't be afraid. They're such wonderful people."

"Alright. Let's go."

Before William had a chance to ring the bell, June opened the door. "Well, hello. At long last I finally get a chance to see what this beautiful girl looks like." Mary blushed. After all, she didn't know if she was beautiful or not. June continued, "William, I don't know how you lucked out like this."

William felt very proud when June said that. June grabbed hold of Mary's arm and led her to a chair to sit down.

"I hope I'm not causing you any trouble," Mary said to June.

"Oh don't be silly. It's a pleasure having you here. We've heard so much about you from William. I'm glad he had the sense to finally ask you to dinner. It gets pretty tiresome living in a house full of men. I enjoy having a woman to talk to for a change. Don't get me wrong, I love them all. But what chance does any woman have against four males?"

"I can surely understand that. We women have to stick together, too."

Then little Ed asked, "Are you William's girlfriend?"

"I certainly hope so."

Then June added, "Why don't you go and wash up for dinner?"

As soon as little Ed left the room, William said, "June, I have something to tell you. I'm going to be leaving you and Ed. Mary and I are going to live together a while and see how it works out. If it does, then we're going to get married."

"I don't think that's such good news that you're leaving us. But I am happy for the both of you."

Then Ed popped up and said, "You mean, I'm going to lose my buddy? I guess that's alright. Maybe I'll be gaining a sister, if you two get married. Just remember one thing, if you have a son, I'd like to be his godfather."

William was speechless, he'd never even thought about having any children. It was the furthest thought from his mind.

"I don't know about having any children," said Mary. "But if God does bless us with a child, you can be sure you'll be the godfather."

William spoke up. "I don't count on God. It seems he punishes the good and rewards the bad."

"Now, William," Mary said, "that isn't right to say."

Then she realized that William had never spoken of any church or God. "I may not be able to see, but I can feel the

25

beauty of flowers and appreciate the sound of laughter. Just like in this house, there's all kinds of love in it. I'm not mad at God because I can't see. If he took my soul, then I'd have a right to be mad. But I can still love."

"I had a nurse once tell me something like that -- that I was lucky to have only lost my sight because there was a man on another floor in the hospital that had lost his soul. Did God punish him for going to war?"

June quickly said dinner was ready. She, Ed and William waited until Mary was seated at the table. Then June grabbed Ed's arm and led him back into the living room. June said, "Ed, sometimes you can be a real ass."

"What did I do?"

"You know they wouldn't be able to have any children. It's different with us. Only one of us is blind. But both of them, how would they ever care for a child?"

"I guess that was a dumb thing to say, but you never know."

At the dinner table, Ed told William that his brother-in-law would help move his things to Mary's house.

"You know," added Mary, "you and your family are pretty nice people. William has told me many times about how kind you are to him. I can't see things, that's true, but I sure can feel kindness."

After they'd finished dinner, they returned to the living room. Mary told them a little about herself. She said she'd never been happier since she'd met William, but she knew she was second to another.

June and Ed both thought she was referring to Elizabeth, but actually it was hockey.

"Well," asked Ed, "how soon before you're going to be leaving us, William?"

Before William had a chance to answer, Mary replied, "As soon as possible, I hope."

"It's Saturday tomorrow," answered Ed. "I'll call Mel in the morning."

"That would be great," said William. "It's not that I'm anxious to leave all of you. I mean I'll miss you and the boys and June. I love you all so much. But you know how it is when

26

you've found someone to love. I think I've found someone who will love me as much as I love her."

Mary felt elated. This was the first time she'd heard William say how much he loved her.

Ed suggested tactfully, "What about your mother? You're already on her shit list. You haven't called or written her in a couple months."

"I'll let her know myself. I'll call her. Listen, can I ask you another favor. I'd like to still have my mail come here, if you don't mind."

"Of course," said June. She glanced in Ed's direction and suggested, "Come on, Ed, why don't you help me with the dishes?"

"I'll help you with them," replied Mary.

"No, thanks. Ed helps me all the time."

"What are you talking about?" asked Ed. "I've never done dishes in my life!"

"Well then, it's about time you learned." June grabbed Ed's arm and led him into the kitchen. She continued, "Honestly, Ed, sometimes, I could crown you. Don't you know those two would like to be alone for a while."

"Why didn't I think of that?"

In the living room, Mary spoke. "William, I hope this works out for us. You know, June and Ed are such wonderful people. You're leaving a really nice home."

"Don't worry about it. It's going to work out for us."

"But I get the feeling you're unsure."

"Why do you say that?"

"Oh, it's nothing."

"No, there's a 'something.' What's wrong?"

"Why do you want your mail delivered here? Do you have a secret girlfriend or something?"

William grinned. "No, there just one woman I'm worried about. That's my mother. I don't want her to fly out here and cause me trouble."

"What kind of trouble could she cause?"

"She wants to live my life for me. I need no interference in our world."

Mary glowed with the realization that she was Number One in William's life. The concern about mail faded away.

"By the way, I'm going to ask Ed if he'll let me take the bed in my room. Other than that, all I have is my clothes and a few pictures." Even though William no longer could see them, the pictures were treasured memories from earlier times when he played hockey and were proof of past accomplishments.

"I have an extra bed. I'm sleeping in my father's bed. You can sleep in my old bed. Mary added softly, "I love you, William."

William was startled. He leaned over and kissed Mary and ran his fingers through her hair. Just then a voice called out, "I hope you two are decent, cause here I come!"

William and Mary both jumped away from each other quickly. Who else but Ed could have broken up a scene like this. Ed could sure be funny at times, after all he couldn't see if they were decent or not.

When June came into the living room, she said to Ed, "Can't you leave these two alone? You're like an old mother hen!"

"That's alright," responded Mary. "I think I'd better be leaving soon. Would you mind taking me home, June?"

"It's early yet," Ed said.

"No, really," replied Mary. "I have a lot of things to do."

An impish grin spread across Ed's face as he asked, "What do you have to do? Wash the windows and dust the furniture so William can see you're a great housekeeper?"

They all started laughing.

"No, really," Mary replied, "I'd like to get the house and everything straightened up before William comes over tomorrow."

"Of course," said June, "I'll get our coats."

William called out, "Get my coat, too. Would you, June?"

"Why don't you stay and talk to Ed," said Mary. "We'll be together tomorrow."

"Alright," William whispered as he kissed her on the forehead, "till tomorrow then."

As June was driving, Mary asked, "June, do you think we're doing the right thing? I mean, I know it will be good for me, but what about William? I'm so happy, but I can't help but feel that something might go wrong. I love William very much, but you see I'm only twenty-two years old. I've never been alone with a man before, if you know what I mean. I'm afraid I won't know what I'm supposed to do."

June smiled. "Don't worry about that, Mary. William is a man. Believe it or not, sometimes they can be just as shy as a woman. Believe me, they like being held and kissed just like you or me. You might even have to coax him a little, but it will come in time."

"Well, tonight William said he was going to ask Ed if he would bring his bed over. I know we've only known each a short time, but I would like to have him sleep with me. Is that being too forward?"

"It's funny you should mention that because when Ed was in the service, I think that's the thing I missed the most, I hated sleeping alone."

"I've never slept with anyone before. But I hear other women at the hospital talking about all their romances. I could never come right out and ask William, but I want to know what it's like."

Just then they pulled up in front of Mary's house. June giggled and said, "I've got an idea that I think will work."

Mary escorted June on a tour of the house. June complimented Mary, "What a lovely house."

"But it's always been a sad house. When my father was alive, I stumbled over many beer cans and bottles. I'm not complaining. But alcohol really ate him up. He lost my mom and I was less than a whole child. He always wanted a child to play baseball or any sport with. I really don't think it mattered if it was a boy or girl, as long as he could have had someone to fulfill his dreams. I wasn't able to. I guess as his penance to me, he left me this house, looking for my forgiveness. He didn't know that I could forgive him without the house.

"When William said tonight that God has punished him, it was what my father often said. But at least my father had my aunt, even if she is a nun. She was an angel who looked out for both of us. He hated hearing her preaching and he'd never say she was right. But yet he took me to church every Sunday."

"You have an aunt who's a nun?"

"Yes, she's at the mother-house in Mokena. She's a pharmacist. I guess that's why I chose a career in the medical profession. When I was a little girl, I even thought about being a nun. As much as my father and her argued, my father always sobered up and took me down there to enjoy their softball games. Just being with my father made me feel closer to him because it was sports. Those are some of my happiest memories."

"Did you ever tell William this?"

"No, June. He tells me what a hockey player he was. As he talks, I can feel the hurt that's inside him. He'll never know I wished I could have been an athlete, too. But for a different reason. I would have loved to please my father."

June felt herself becoming saddened so she asked Mary to show her the rest of the house, stopping at Mary's bedroom when she was a little girl. June took the covers off the bed and rolled up the mattress. She put it on the back porch. "Well now," chuckled June, "that's taken care of. Now William has no choice as to where he'll sleep, unless he wants to sleep on springs. All you have to do is say you forgot about the mattress and you can sort of suggest that you'd be glad to share you bed. If he's any kind of a man, how can he refuse such a kind offer. Right?"

Mary and June giggled.

"Do you suppose if William and I got married, we could have a child. Or is that talking out of my head?"

"I honestly don't know what to say about that. There's a tremendous amount of responsibility with a child. Let me say one thing that if you and William do get married, that's a decision the two of you would have to make together. Don't let anyone interfere with your decision, especially William's mother."

"I get this feeling, June, that there's going to be a problem with his mother."

"Honey, she's just an old busy-body who wants to dominate William. But he isn't going to let that happen."

June wanted to get off the subject because she didn't have the answers.

"Where is you phone, Mary?"

"I don't have one. I never had anyone that I really cared to talk to."

"We're going to have to change that. After all, I'll be calling you to talk about our love lives."

"I've never been so happy before. But there is one thing I'd like to ask you, June. What does William look like. Is he handsome?"

"He is very handsome."

"Now tell me the truth, June. I'd like to know, am I pretty enough for William?"

"I don't know how else to put this, but if William could see, and there were ten pretty girls in this room, I'm sure he'd pick you out."

"Really? That makes me happy."

"Mary, I've got to be getting back now. We'll talk again real soon."

When June returned home, the four guys were wrestling on the floor.

"It's time for you kids to get to bed," said June.

"Is Uncle William really leaving?" asked little Ed.

Tommy burst out crying. "I don't want Uncle William to go."

"He's only moving a few blocks away. You'll still be able to see him. Now let's hop into bed. Come on, Ed, why don't you put your kids to bed? I'd like to talk to William for a minute."

As soon as they were alone, William asked June what she thought of Mary.

"I think she's a wonderful girl."

"Do you think everything will be okay?"

"Things should be just fine, but I wouldn't call your mother just yet. Let's see how things go for a while. You're taking a big step, but I think it's a good one."

June didn't know that William had no intention of calling his mother. "I think you're right, June. You know if I hadn't come

31

here to live with you and Ed, I would never have met Mary. I just can't thank you both enough."

"It's me who should be thanking you. I don't think Ed would have left that hospital without you. He put up a big front, but actually I know he was afraid to come home to me and the kids."

"Say, June, I'd like to ask you a question about Mary. Is she pretty? What does she really look like?"

June had to smile at hearing those questions again.

William continued, "It doesn't matter, but I'm just curious. I would like to know."

"She's a pretty woman. I'm not just telling you that to make you feel good."

"Thanks, thanks a lot."

William went to bed that night, impatient for morning to arrive. Meanwhile, June kept talking to Ed even though he was half asleep. "You know, Ed, we're going to have to help them as much as we can. I think one of the first things is to get a phone installed."

"And what am I supposed to do?"

"You can talk with William about the facts of life."

"You've got to be joking."

"Well, smart guy, has he ever talked to you about women very much?"

"No, come to think of it. He's said very little. We talk mostly about hockey."

"You know, Ed, don't repeat this to William, but Mary doesn't know very much about sex and what's expected of her. I can give her a few facts, but you'll have to brief William. This could be a very touchy thing for Mary."

Then June went on to tell Ed about what she and Mary had done to the mattress. Ed couldn't stop laughing and said, "And you're worried about how they're going to get along?"

"Sleeping together and having sex are not the same thing, Ed. Remember, this will be Mary's first time."

Ed couldn't stop laughing and June had to tell him to shut up or he'd wake the kids.

Saturday morning came quickly. June was the first one up. She was more excited than when she went to pick up William and Ed from Buffalo. It was almost a year to the day since they had come home to Chicago. She called Mel, getting him out of bed. He said he'd be happy to help them move William.

June had to take the boys to hockey at Rainbo, so she left Ed and William at the breakfast table, hoping Ed would have a little talk with William. As soon as June left with the kids, Ed said, "Now you listen to me. You give her about a week. Then you buy her s see-through negligee, and act like you're going to rape her." Ed could barely contain his laughter.

"What the hell are you talking about?" asked William.

"I'm talking about you and Mary."

Then William started laughing, too. "First of all, why the hell would I buy a see-through negligee?"

"You've got to use your imagination, William."

"I don't know about you, Ed. Sometimes I wonder if you're really blind or just cheating the government. Don't worry about me. I've been on a few jobs. I know what to do."

Actually though, William was ashamed to admit to Ed that he'd never been around much. He'd spent so much time playing hockey when all his friends were out running around, that he'd had very little experiences with the opposite sex.

Mel was ringing the doorbell. Ed answered it. Mel said, "How you doing hero?"

"Okay, I guess."

"June said your buddy is leaving you."

"Yeah, he found this broad and now he's got hot pants. No kidding, she's really a nice girl. William likes her a lot, so what can I say?"

Just then June pulled up in her car, she'd only dropped off the kids and came back to pack. William had almost everything ready. It didn't take long to get it into Mel's car. They were on their way. Five minutes later they were at Mary's house. She'd been waiting anxiously and had coffee already made. They sat down and talked a short while when June said they'd better be leaving because she had to go back to the rink and get the kids. June told Mary she'd see about having a phone installed that

33

next week because they'd have a lot to talk about to each other. Mary knew what she meant.

CHAPTER THREE

After everyone left, William and Mary were a little nervous, but it didn't take long for them to relax. Mary made them lunch, and later dinner, as if she'd been doing it for years. They listened to the radio as Mary showed William the books she had in Braille. They talked for hours on end. Finally Mary said, "William, I'm getting a little sleepy. Aren't you? Maybe we should call it a day."

"That's a good idea. It's been a tiring day for both of us."

Mary grabbed his arm. "Let me show you to your bed."

In her former bedroom, she led him to the bed. "Why don't you sit down for a minute?"

William sat down - right on the hard springs. Mary sat down beside him and exclaimed, "Oh my God, there's no mattress! I forgot William, I threw out the mattress a long time ago." She was silent for a moment before she got up enough nerve to say, "If you don't mind, William, my bed is rather large, I'm sure the both of us could share it until we can get a mattress for you."

"I don't mind at all," said William as he smiled to himself.

"Well good, let's go down the hall and I'll show you my room." As they walked down the hall they were both smiling to themselves.

Mary showed him around the room, led him to the bed, and said, "I think you'll be comfortable here on this side. I'll take the other side. Why don't you get undressed while I lock up the house?"

"Fine, but do you know where Mel left my bags so I can get out my pajamas?"

"Oh sure, I'll get them for you."

Mary brought him his bags and then went about the house checking the doors. She was thinking about something June had mentioned - that men were sometimes more bashful than women and sometimes women had to make the first move. When Mary got back to the bedroom William was already in bed. She undressed quickly, leaving on her bra and panties. As she laid down, she could tell that William must have been lying on the very edge of his side of the bed. It was a boundary line, she became frightened for a moment and then she said, "Are you okay, William? Are you there?"

"I'm here. I feel very happy. How about you?"

Mary didn't answer. She rolled over and with her hands felt his face. Then she kissed him. William moved his arms and put them around her. He felt her bare skin. From that moment, neither one of them needed any guidance from anybody. They both knew what they were doing. For the first time, they both felt the beauty of a sexual relationship together.

Time flew after their first night together. They were happy, except William complained that Mary and June were on the phone too much. William didn't like sharing Mary with anybody. Ed and June came over at least once a week to visit. The boys bicycled over to see if they could do anything for them. Ed was still meeting them at the bus stop each morning and evening. William had June write a couple of letters to his mother. Ada didn't know that William wasn't living with June and Ed.

Between William's pension and Mary's salary, they were able to make it fine financially. They managed to save a few dollars.

One evening as William and Mary were sitting on the couch, he asked her, "Mary are you happy with our arrangement?"

"Oh yes, I've never been so happy in all my life."

"I didn't exactly mean that. I know I've never been so happy, either. I meant, don't you think we ought to get married?"

Mary hugged him tightly, "Oh yes, yes."

"What about this weekend?"

"That's not enough time."

William convinced her that he wanted to make an honest woman out of her now, not later. It didn't take much to change her mind.

Mary called June to tell her the good news. June and Ed were almost as excited as Mary and William.

June and Mary were busy the next few days. June took Mary shopping for a dress and accessories. Mary told her

36

supervisor at the hospital she was getting married and would be taking off a couple weeks. Her co-workers quickly planned a bridal shower.

June decided she'd better contact William's mother. When Ada heard the news, she was none too happy. June explained to her how happy William was and this was probably the best thing that could have happened to him. Ada thought her son was making a big mistake. June begged her not to destroy their elated spirits. Ada agreed to fly in for the wedding, probably on Saturday, the day before they were to be married. Ada asked if there was anything she could do to help, but June assured her that everything was under control. The cake, food, and liquor had been ordered. June had contacted her own priest who received permission from the bishop to hold the wedding services in Mary's home. Thank God for June, she'd thought of everything.

William's mother arrived the day before the wedding. June and Ed picked her up from the airport. Ada and June talked all the way home. Ada didn't wholeheartedly accept the idea of William marrying another blind person. June convinced her that William was ecstatic and very much in love with Mary. When they arrived at Mary's house, Mary answered the bell and said, "Come in."

June made the introductions. Ada smiled politely, but her voice revealed the apprehension she felt about her son's marriage. She knew she'd never get him to return to Ogdensburg. And to top it off, this was not the woman she would have chosen for her son. Mary was speechless. She didn't know what to say when William's mother said, "My you certainly are a lovely looking girl, Mary."

"Why thank you very much," a startled Mary answered.

"I hear you're going to take my son away from me, but I guess every mother has to expect that."

"Oh, Mrs. LaBuld, I'm not taking him away from you. We can both love him." Mary reached out for Ada's arm, and Ada politely hugged her. "Thank you for being so kind," said Mary as she wept a little.

"Where is that good looking son of mine?"

Mary called out, "William, you have someone very special here who would like to see you."

William guessed that his mother had arrived. "Mom, is that you?"

As Ada looked at William, tears welled in her eyes. He did indeed look happier than she'd seen him in such a long time. "It's me, son," said Ada as she walked over and held him. "I'm so happy for both of you. I know you'll be happy. Mary looks like a real nice girl." She bit her lip as she tried to exude warmth. But she knew she'd never be able to have her son for herself or convince him to return home.

"I know, Mom, I know."

June and Ed left shortly after lunch to give Mary time to become acquainted with her new mother-in-law.

In the afternoon, Mary's house was invaded by a company of ants - all kinds of workers, including June's children. Ada reluctantly pitched in, but was tickled when Tommy addressed her as Grandma. He explained to her that she was such a nice lady and it was great to have three grandmas. Ada's heart was warming towards the children. She overheard Tommy say to Eddie, "Wouldn't it be great if Aunt Mary and Uncle William had a baby boy so we could make him a goalie."

Eddie remarked, "Yeah, Aunt Mary said she'd liked to have a baby."

Ada mellowed further at the thought of being a grandmother. The possessive bitterness in her heart was melted when she heard the boys' conversation. Now she helped herself to the open bottle of wine and replaced the scowl on her face with a smile reminiscent of the cat who swallowed the canary. Her thoughts were interrupted by the doorbell's ringing. More ants arrived: Sister Richard and her friend Sister Bertha popped in to see if there was anything they could do to help. Mary warmly greeted the two nuns and introduced them. The adults didn't know how to respond to the nuns, the atmosphere became strained. William didn't know if he should shake their hands or what the proper procedure was. Sister Richard good humoredly took the initiative, shook his hand, and said, "It's a pleasure to meet you,

William. How about a hug for your new Aunt?" Sister Bertha didn't want to be left out and she spoke up, "There's one more little nun who wouldn't mind a big hug." Ada was embarrassed to be seen drinking wine in the middle of the afternoon. She meekly explained herself, "I don't normally do this sort of thing, but..."

Sister Richard felt the tension, and asked, "Mary, do you have a little cold beer for your favorite Aunt?"

Mary smiled, "Of course. Sr. Bertha, what can I get for you?"

"Oh, a little glass of that wine Mrs. LaBuld's drinking would be fine."

The ice was broken and the festive mood returned.

Since this was the first time William had met Sr. Richard, she wanted to become better acquainted with him. "I hear you were a hockey player."

Ada proudly interjected, "He was a wonderful hockey player."

William was shocked! This was the first time he had ever heard his mother praise his hockey ability.

Tommy and little Ed heard this, and the next thing Ada knew, she was surrounded on the couch by two little boys telling her all about hockey.

William was eavesdropping on their conversation. He had felt that God had dealt him a bad hand, but today he had four queens. The fifth queen, June, was busy decorating the house.

Everyone, except Ada, returned to organizing the house for the wedding. She couldn't tear herself away from the boys and their hockey tales. When everything was done, Mary was trying to figure out where the nuns and Mrs. LaBuld would sleep that night. June asked the nuns if they'd like to stay at her house.

Ada's voice was heard, "I'll stay at your house, June, so Mary and her Aunt can talk." The boys clapped their hands. "Can Grandma LaBuld really spend the night? Please, Mom, she knows hockey!"

Mrs. LaBuld felt wanted and loved. She needed to pay back the kindness and happiness she felt this day.

39

It suddenly dawned on William, that if the nuns were going to spend the night, Mary must have another mattress. He realized that his shy queen had duped him that first night.

That evening, as William and Mary laid in bed, without saying a word to each other, they both knew they were at the top of the rainbow.

The next day was like a mad house. It had been years since Mary's house had held so many people. Mary's friends from the hospital were there, as well as friends and teachers from the Lighthouse. The boys, Ada, and the nuns were assisting June in last minute preparations. Mel felt important, even though he wasn't best man, he had to help William get dressed. June helped Mary. Soon the time arrived. As William and Mary entered the living room, assisted by Ed and June, a silence fell over everyone. It was a beautiful, touching scene. Even the priest himself had never felt anything like it before. As Mary and William said "I do," especially the part for better or worse, there wasn't a dry eye in the room. Ada especially felt the depth of their love. She thought to herself how relieved she was that it hadn't worked out for William and Elizabeth and now he had found happiness and love with Mary. In her heart, when she compared Elizabeth and Mary, Elizabeth came in a pale second, Mary was truly first class. After the ceremony, everyone made a toast and gathered around for the opening of the wedding presents.

Ada was given the honor of opening the gifts. There were many lovely presents. Everything went smoothly, until Ada opened the one gift that shocked the guests. Inside the package was a very lacy, see-through negligee. The guests in the room were silently containing their giggles and laughs.

"What's all the silence?" William asked.

Ada was so embarrassed she couldn't speak. Ed spoke up, "That's got to be the negligee I bought."

Even June was shocked. Then William started laughing and everyone joined in. Even though Sr. Richard and Sr. Bertha were astonished, they were laughing, too. Mary's face was flushed.

June said, "Why it's beautiful, Ed. Where ever did you get it?"

"That's a secret!" He giggled.

During the rest of the evening, Ed was joking and telling his usual unbelievable stories. He even told Mary's friends that William had met Mary in a strip tease joint - that Mary was a stripper in the evenings. The guests thought Ed was funny enough to be a comedian, after all, not every blind person could be so humorous about blindness. The priest wasn't too keen on Ed, but everyone else enjoyed his jokes. The reception lasted until about 1:00 A.M. After the guests had gone, June, Ed, Ada, William and Mary sat and talked a while.

"Just think," said Ed to William, "I was your best man. That's like the blind leading the blind."

They all laughed. Mary responded, "I certainly hope not. I intend to make him very happy."

"I'm just kidding," said Ed. "I was proud to be best man. June was just as proud to stand up for Mary."

"You know something, June," began Ada, "you're like a miracle worker. You've decorated the house and seen to all the details for the wedding. I think I'm jealous of Mary; not for taking my son, but for having such a wonderful friend." Ada cried tears of joy as she hugged June. "When William came to live with you, I was hurt. But now I realize it was the best decision he could have made. You've taken care of my son and given him a chance for happiness that he would not have had anywhere else."

Ada turned to Mary, "Mary, my son found a rare gem when he met you. But I am hurt - I don't want you to call me Mrs. LaBuld. Please call me Mom." Ada warmly hugged Mary. "As William's love has grown for you, I know mine will, too."

Next, Ada spoke about her special relationship with Tommy and Eddie. "I hope one day, I'll be a grandmother. The boys have shown me how children can make my world complete."

The newlyweds felt a bit embarrassed. Mary changed the subject. "June, how can we ever thank you for everything the both of you have done?"

41

"Don't be silly. But I'm getting a little tired, so why don't we go home? Ada is going to spend a few more days with Ed and me, that way the two of you can be alone on your little honeymoon."

Mary and William weren't going anywhere for a honeymoon. They were going to enjoy being in their house: sleep till they felt like getting up and doing whatever they wanted.

Alone at last, William asked, "Well, don't you think it's about time?"

"Time for what?"

"Why it's time for the groom to make out with his wife. In fact, if you resist I'll just have to rape you." They both giggled. "But first, there's one thing we have to do."

"What's that, William?"

"We're going to go back outside so I can carry you over the threshold."

"Are you serious?"

"I certainly am," said William as he grabbed her hand, led her outside, and shut the door behind him. He picked her up in his arms and went to open the door, but it had locked. "Mary, you're not going to believe this, but I think we're locked out. You don't happen to have a key hidden under the welcome mat, do you?"

"No."

"Well, you'll have to wait here. I'll get some help."

"What are you going to do?"

"Don't worry. I'll find someone." William started to walk down the street, but it was difficult without his cane. He heard someone coming down the street and asked, "Can you help me?"

It was only a drunk who didn't pay any attention to him.

William kept on walking down the sidewalk until he tripped and fell over a big crack. William felt someone tightly grab his arm and say, "Okay, buddy, let's go with me."

"I'm blind," explained William, "please help me."

Then the man shone a flashlight towards his eyes and said, "Why you really are blind. What are you doing out here this late alone?"

William proceeded to tell him the whole story. It turned out the man who found him was a police officer on patrol with his partner in the area. The officers helped him into their patrol car and drove him back home. They decided the only thing they could do was break a window and climb through. Then Mary remembered that June had an extra key. The officers drove them to June's house.

While Mary related the whole story to June, Ed sat in the chair laughing his head off. June gave Mary the extra key and the police officers were kind enough to offer them a ride back to their house. When they finally got there, William and Mary thanked them for being so helpful. The policemen drove away saying that this was a new one on them.

William put the key in the door, picked up Mary, and said, "I'm still carrying you over the threshold."

Once safely inside the house, Mary felt a bump on William's head. She said, "What happened? You didn't tell me you got hurt. What happened to you?"

"I fell, that's all."

Mary started crying. "Oh William, I don't know what I'd do if anything happened to you."

"Don't worry, nothing's going to happen to me." He thought to himself, "Damn, it's lousy being blind." He tried to cheer up Mary. "Hey this is our honeymoon. I want you to get dressed in that negligee and model it for me. I'm going to give you five minutes to get ready and into that bed, or I'm going to make you right here."

Mary started smiling. "Only if you'll go with me right now."

As soon as they got into bed and William began kissing Mary, reality set in and Mary said, "William, where did you put the key?"

"Is that all you can think of now?"

"Of course not." But as William began to make love to her, she just couldn't forget about that key. She didn't remember him taking it out of the lock. "Are you sure you have the key?"

"Damn it, now that I think about it, maybe I left it in the lock."

43

William got up to look, he knew Mary was worried and as he snuck out to look for it, who should be passing by but the same two police officers. There stood William, without a stitch of clothes, taking the key out of the lock.

The officers looked at each other and said, "I don't believe it!" as they shook their heads.

William got back to the bedroom quickly and hopped into bed telling Mary that the key had been on the living room table all along.

CHAPTER FOUR

Mary and William's life together was wonderful. William was continuing at the Lighthouse, and the three blind mice met at the bus stop each day. Mary was enjoying married life, too. She was still working at the hospital. All she ever talked about was her husband. Tommy and Eddie came over to their house and told their hockey stories which William enjoyed. Little did the boys imagine how frustrated he felt.

In June of 1969, Mary phoned June and told her she was worried, she hadn't had her period in two months. "What do you suppose is the matter with me?"

June thought about it for a minute. "Do you suppose you could be pregnant?"

"I was hoping you'd ask me that. I'm going to the doctor tomorrow and have a test taken. You know, June, if I am pregnant it would make me very happy. But I don't know how I'd be able to take care of a baby. Besides, I don't know what William would say."

"Well, Mary, you'll never know until you tell him. Don't worry about taking care of the baby, I'd be glad to help with that."

The next day, Mary kept her appointment with her doctor. He suggested a pregnancy test, but she'd have to wait a couple days for the results. The days went by and Mary stopped off in his office. The waiting patients were wondering why a blind woman would want to get pregnant, and they began whispering amongst themselves. Finally the nurse called Mary and took her into the doctor's office.

The doctor came right out and said, "Mrs. LaBuld, the pregnancy test came out positive. You are pregnant. Now Mrs. LaBuld, I don't usually say things like this to my patients. But under the circumstances, if you want, I'll arrange for you to have an abortion."

Mary began crying. "We want the baby, doctor."

"But how will you be able to take care of it?"

"I have a friend who will help me. The only thing I'm worried about is would the baby be born blind. You see, I was born blind, but my husband wasn't. He was wounded in the war. If we had a child, would the baby be born blind? Is it hereditary?"

"The chances are so slim of your child being born blind that I wouldn't even concern myself with that. For now, there's nothing to worry about. We can look forward to a strong, healthy baby in January."

Mary's emotions were ranging from happiness at the very idea of being pregnant to apprehension of the awesome responsibilities of caring for a child. She looked forward to the baby, yet was scared of the future. Mary knew she had to tell William right away.

As Mary and William were lying in bed that evening, Mary asked, "William, if you could have anything, what would you want?"

"I'd want to play hockey again."

"What would be your second choice?"

"There's nothing else I want. But I'm not complaining. I have you, I love you. I don't need anything more."

"Not even a son or daughter?"

"Well, that would be fantastic. But how could we? It's hard enough for sighted people to raise a child. How could we? It's just like hockey. People think it's easy to score. It's not that easy."

"Well, honey, you scored. And you scored a goal. That's an awful powerful stick you carry!"

"Are you telling me you're pregnant?"

"You can bet your ice skates on that."

William took his arm from around her shoulder and stood up. He started laughing, and smiling and jumping around. He shouted, "I'm going to play again. I'm going to play again."

Mary couldn't understand what had gotten into him. Finally he laid down again, resting his head on Mary's stomach. She felt enormous tears coming from William's eyes.

"God has been good to me," he said. "I'm going to have a son to play hockey."

"Suppose it's not a son," said Mary as the tears flowed from her eyes, too.

He held onto her a little harder and said, "God is going to take care of us, I know he will. I know we're going to have a son. Think positive, Mary."

"I will, William, I will."

William fell asleep that night on Mary's stomach.

As Mary laid quietly, she was smiling for more than one reason. This was the first time she had heard William talk about his faith and trust in God. She knew things would work out because William's belief in his Lord had returned.

They awakened early the next morning, William couldn't wait to call Ed and tell him the good news. Ed acted surprised on the phone, but June had already told him. Ed and June were waiting to see how William would react. This was the best present, besides Mary, that William had ever had in his life, and he was sure it was going to be a boy.

William and Mary had lots of preparations to make. June again said she would be thrilled to baby-sit if Mary decided to return to work after the baby was born.

The expectant parents called Ada with the wonderful announcement. Ada was delighted. Mary explained that June would be watching the baby after he was born. Ada didn't want June encroaching on her grandmotherly rights. She decided to come to Chicago and stay with Mary at least until the baby was born. Ada reminded William that babies had a way of not obeying their parents - "he" might very well be a "she."

Mary and William thought about naming the baby. William did not want him named Junior - he would be his own unique person. But picking the right name would be difficult. Mary suggested they pick a name that reflected their hopes that he would be a winner, a champion, a victor. Suddenly it registered - Victor. The more William thought about it, the more he liked the name. Days later, from the back of his mind, William remembered the name Victor Wolf from his stay in the Veterans Hospital. Wasn't he a hockey player, too?

Time went by quickly. All William's friends at the Lighthouse listened to him talking about his wife giving him a son. His friends hoped and prayed William would have a son, they didn't want any disappointments for him. He made Mary quit work because he didn't want her exposed to any radiation.

Ada arrived from New York to stay with them until the baby was born. Ada got to like Mary more and more. She was delighted she was going to be a grandmother. Remembering when William had been in the hospital and the way he was, she never dreamed all these wonderful things would happen to him.

It was Jan. 14, 1970, when Mary started into labor.

June, Ed, Ada, and William drove her to Cook County Hospital where she had asked to go - she had worked there for so many years she felt she would be more comfortable among people she knew. The nurse took Mary to the maternity floor. After the doctor checked her over, William was allowed to go into the labor room with her. Mary was crying and said to William, "I hope God isn't blind, William. I hope He loves us enough to give us a healthy baby."

"I know He will. He will, believe me."

The nurse came in and told William it was time they took her to the delivery room. An orderly helped William back to the waiting room where June, Ed, and Ada were. The waiting room held two other expectant fathers. Everyone waited, silently praying that a healthy baby would soon enter the world. One of the other men asked William, "Is a relative of yours having a baby?"

William smiled. "Not exactly, but my wife is."

The room was silent again as June and Ada smiled.

By 10:00 P.M., the other two men had left, having become new fathers. William was getting worried. June and Ada fell asleep in their chairs. Finally Ed and William did, too.

At 2:00 A.M., a nurse began shaking William's shoulder. "Mr. LaBuld, you have a brand new, very healthy, baby boy."

William was speechless.

"Can we see the baby?" asked June.

"Of course. Come with me." She led them down the hall to the nursery and held up the baby to the window.

Ada explained to William every detail about the baby, and then thought to herself, "How awful, he'll never know what his own son looks like."

William was proud of what he heard, but in his mind he was visualizing just a boy and a hockey stick.

Then William thought about Mary and asked, "My wife, how is she? Is she alright?"

"She's doing fine," replied the nurse. "You can go to her room now if you like."

"I'd like that very much."

The nurse led him to Mary's room. She was quietly resting. He bent down, kissed her softly on the lips, and whispered, "I love you. Thank you."

Mary rolled over, opened her eyes, and murmured, "And you think a hockey game is exhausting! The nurses told me he's a beautiful, healthy boy. Who does he look like?"

William started laughing, "You're asking me?"

The nurse in the room settled the question by answering, "He looks like both of you."

After a short visit, June, Ed, and Ada walked the proud father down the hall to the elevator. William felt ten feet tall. The whole world was beautiful.

As they were going home, Ed was ribbing William. "The baby's wiener is so long, it's going to take four doctors to circumcise him. He's got so many pimples on his face that you're going to go broke buying Clearasil."

"Knock it off, Ed," warned June. "William, that is one handsome baby."

"I still think we'd better find him a hooker before they circumcise him. I'm not saying anymore."

William, exhausted by Mary's long ordeal, was laughing and crying at the same time.

49

Mary had to stay in the hospital longer than expected. She had difficulties during the birth. June took William to the hospital every day. Finally the day came when he could take Mary and Victor home. Waiting at their house to see the baby were friends, as well as Connie and Mel, and Sr. Richard and Sr. Bertha. The baby was handed back and forth from one person to another like a sack of potatoes.

Sr. Richard volunteered to change his diapers. As she did so, Victor decided to be a Buckingham Fountain and squirted on her habit.

Suddenly, there was a screech. Ed yelled, "It's a miracle. It's a fountain of holy water."

Sr. Richard turned and innocently replied, "No, it's just a wet habit." That remark got more laughs than all of Ed's jokes put together.

Finally Ada put the baby in her room in the bassinet and stayed with him until he went to sleep. Mary was exhausted and she laid down. She thought to herself what she'd said to the doctor right after she delivered. Her first words were, "Doctor, will the baby be able to see?"

"There's nothing wrong. You have a fine healthy baby boy," the doctor replied. Those words were magic to Mary's ears.

It turned out that William's mother decided to sell her house in Ogdensburg and stay with William and Mary. They were pleased with Ada's decision. June was glad for them, but a bit disappointed. A jealousy developed between June and Ada. June was over at the house every chance she got so she could play with the baby.

For the next four years, Victor was an unruly little boy. Grandma Ada convinced William and Mary into enrolling Victor in nursery school so her precocious grandson would be a step ahead of the other children when he started kindergarten. But there were problems.

Victor was a highly intelligent boy. Eddie and Tommy were like his older brothers. Uncle Ed gave Victor his sense of humor. The only drawback was it was an adult sense of humor. One day, Victor stood in front of his class at "Show and Tell Time" and recited his favorite nursery rhyme:

Mary had a little lamb,

Its fleece was white as snow,

And everywhere that Mary went,

She stepped in lamb doo-doo.

Grandma Ada didn't think it was so funny when she picked up her grandson and had to explain to the teacher why Victor knew such a rhyme.

Not only was Victor a poet, but he was also learning to ice skate. Tommy and Eddie took him along to Rainbo for the public skating sessions. When the boys came home, they'd tell Mary and William what a great little skater Victor was. William and Mary were pleased with the progress reports, but they truly didn't know if Victor was good or if the boys were simply trying to cheer them up. William asked Ada to go with the boys and check out Victor's ability.

The day Ada saw Victor skate she couldn't contain the flood of tears of past memories. She was reliving her son's childhood and his early skating experiences. He had the same determined look on his face. He never cried when he fell down. He seemed to fly on his skates. Ada realized William had been right. She promised herself she'd see her grandson skate just like his father. She saw the Pro Shop and after the session was over, took the boys in and brought Victor every piece of hockey equipment that was available. But being a fair grandmother, she also bought her other two grandsons the equipment they needed. It was better than Christmas.

Johnny, the Pro Shop manager, was himself a generous man. Even he couldn't believe all the equipment this woman was buying. He asked Ada, "How old is your grandson?"

"Four, but he'll be five in January."

Johnny was disappointed. "Damn, I wish he was five already. We have this new instructor who was a pro hockey player, but he accepts only students five and up."

Tommy burst out, "I hear he's mean."

Johnny said, "He's not mean, he's strict."

51

Ada hesitatingly asked, "Could I meet this instructor?"

Johnny felt obligated because of all the equipment this woman had purchased. He went to the public address system and paged, "Junior, please come to the Pro Shop."

Ada thought, "What a strange name for someone in charge of the clinic."

Five minutes later the Coach appeared. When he walked in, it wasn't hard for Ada to know he was the Coach. But she was taken aback by the unshaven face, blood shot eyes, and strong smell of alcohol on his breath.

Johnny introduced him to Ada as the boys silently stood in fear and awe.

"What can I do for you?"

"This nice young man told me you teach the clinics. But you start the boys only at five years. Would there be any way for you to take my grandson? He's not five yet. But in my judgment, I think he has the potential now."

The Coach rolled his eyes. He'd heard this so many times before. "Do you know that much about hockey?"

"I certainly do," Ada strongly replied. "Where I'm from, the day they get out of their cribs, they have ice skates on their feet."

Once again the Coach rolled his eyes. "Where are you from, ma'am?'

"Ogdensburg, New York. My son was one of the greatest players to come out of there, until he lost his eyes in Vietnam."

"You say he's blind now?"

"Yes, but I'm my son's eyes when it comes to my grandson and skating. I've been through raising one hockey star. I know this boy has the ability, just like his father."

Johnny was waiting for the Coach to say no, he'd seen the Coach turn down many pushy parents. But for some reason, the Coach told Ada to lace the boy's skates, he'd take a look at him on the ice.

As the Coach leaned back on the rink's boards, he watched Victor skate. He told the boy, "That's enough," and walked over to Ada.

Ada's heart was pounding. She knew she was bluffing in the Pro Shop, and she knew from Johnny's face that if Victor wasn't good enough or ready, he wouldn't get into the clinic.

"Well, Mrs. LaBuld, I don't think there's going to be any problem here. It looks like those private lessons that he's taken have paid off."

Then Eddie looked at the Coach. "Victor's had no private lessons. My brother and I taught him."

The Coach's eyes looked to Ada, "Is this true?"

"Yes, it is." Ada smiled. "Just remember, his father's from Ogdensburg."

For the first time, the Coach smiled back at her. "You're right, ma'am. It's the water they drink! The great ones do come from Ogdensburg."

Ada thought the Coach was playing with her.

Little Victor looked up and said, "Thank you for letting me come to the clinic, Junior."

The Coach turned to him and said, "Don't you ever call me Junior. I'm the Coach to you."

On the way out of the rink, Eddie mentioned to Grandma, "I think I'd like to have him teach me. Everyone says he's the best."

Grandma LaBuld made a U-turn and went back inside. She caught the Coach before he returned to the ice. "Coach, my other grandsons want to know, do you take kids who play on teams?"

The Coach's eyes glared at Eddie. "Any boy that can teach a four year old to skate like that can certainly put up with me."

Ada signed them up and paid their fees for the year.

Eddie told Grandma on the way out that his mom would pay her back.

Ada said, "Don't worry about it. I've already been paid back. You've done a great job with Victor. This is my gift to you."

When they came home, Ada explained to Mary and William how she told off that Coach and demanded that Victor be allowed in the clinic. But she didn't tell them she was holding her breath the entire time. She also related that the Coach was appalling, but if he'd only shave and clean himself up, he'd be an attractive man. William hugged his mother and through his tear-stained glasses revealed the emotion he felt. Mary also hugged Ada and said, "I'm glad you're with us."

Ada strutted to her room to call Sr. Richard and tell her how she dealt with this Coach and show she got Victor enrolled in the clinic. Since the day of the wedding, Sr. Richard and Ada developed a close relationship. In Ada's mind, Sr. Richard had a direct pipeline to God, and it was through her intervention that William's tragedy had been turned around for him to achieve happiness. Ada also felt Sr. Richard was responsible for her own resulting happiness and contentment. She believed it was through Sr. Richard's prayers that William could once again go to church where an aura of faith and devotion surrounded him even though he couldn't see the crucifix.

As the weeks went by, Ada took the boys to the rink. This kindness gave June and Ed more time together. As Ada watched the boys in the clinic, she was upset by how the Coach treated the kids. He worked them as hard as grown men. She couldn't understand why the kids seemed to enjoy it. Although the Coach patted them on their behinds or backs as praise, he came down especially hard when they made mistakes. It got to the point where she asked Victor if he would like to go somewhere else. Victor adamantly said, "No!"

Ada was shocked one week when she observed a black boy who had been coming to every session to watch the boys on the ice. Many times the Coach skated towards this boy and he ran out of the building. This day, Ada was unnerved when the Coach had Johnny cover the door so the boy couldn't escape. The Coach caught him. The Coach had the other instructors continue the clinic as he left with the boy.

Twenty minutes later, the Coach came back with a fully dressed goalie. Ada stared. It was the black boy. It was obvious this was the first time the boy had been on skates. He was as ungainly as a new born colt. The Coach assigned an instructor to work one-on-one with this boy.

Later Ada heard through the grapevine that the Coach and Johnny had argued with the owner of the rink over this boy.

Johnny was criticized by the owner for donating used equipment. Yet, being manager of the Pro Shop allowed him to be generous to the boy who reminded him of himself when he was a goalie. The owner maintained that every boy had to pay his own way and the Coach couldn't let every stray from the street on the ice. The Coach countered that the pay raise he was about to get should be used for the boy's fees.

Ada didn't understand the Coach's methods. If the Coach was so caring about the boys, then he must have a reason for being so rough on the ice. What distressed her most was the way the Coach treated his own son: ten times harder than the other boys. He had to be perfect. It was ironic that the boy's name was Victor, too.

At night William dreamed of what his son could do on the ice. One Sunday, he asked his mother to take Mary and him with them. Ada never asked why or anything else. Mary, too, thought it was strange, knowing he'd never see his son perform.

Just like the other mothers, Ada usually carried Victor's bag. She was considered a "hockey mom," which although prestigious, meant she was a work horse. But today William enjoyed that honor. As Victor went to the locker room, Ada escorted Mary and William to the bleachers. Ada saw on William's face the same radiance as when he received communion.

Ada alerted William, "He's here, on the ice, skating around."

"You mean Victor's on the ice?"

"No, the Coach. He's just skating around. By the looks of him he had a bad night. He's dressed in a jean jacket and a pair of Levis."

Suddenly the little monsters hit the ice, screaming and yelling as they skated in a big circle around the rink, suggesting a band of Indians surrounding a circle of covered wagons. William sat remembering how he was trained and taught. He was pensive, reflecting that his son would feel and come to know the love of the game he had. The mood was broken when a whistle blew and a voice commanded, "On the line! Sixty second drill!"

The boys immediately went into the program and started skating back and forth. When it was over, the no-nonsense voice of the Coach was heard explaining new techniques as he demonstrated them.

William asked, "Is Victor the fastest?"

Ada answered, "The Coach's son is just a little faster, but he's a year older and has been skating longer."

Mary told William, "It's not who's the fastest. All those boys deserve credit for just being out there. I couldn't stand someone yelling at me like that."

At the end of the session, Ada guided William and Mary down from the bleachers. Mary overheard a little boy talking to his mother, "I'm drunk! The Coach was breathing right in my face. He made me drunk."

Mary wondered as any normal mother, "What kind of person is teaching my son?"

The other parents speculated about the two newcomers: to whom were they related and why would blind people attend a hockey clinic?

When Victor came out of the locker room, he went right to his parents. He excitedly asked, "Did you hear how well I did? That was a hard practice."

Tommy and Eddie explained to Grandma Ada that the Coach was in one of his moods today.

Grandma replied, "Did you learn anything?"

Eddie answered, "The Coach is great. He knows what's going to happen before it happens."

William heard this, "That's because he played the game, Eddie. If I could see, I'd show you some moves of my own."

As the Coach was coming off the ice, Ada showed her mastery of the situation. "Oh, Coach," she yelled out.

He walked over to the group and with a hoarse voice asked, "What can I do for you, Miss Ogdensburg?"

William stifled a smile as he thought, "What has my mother been up to now?"

Ada continued, "I want to introduce you to Victor's father and mother."

First the Coach shook Mary's hand and said, "Glad to make your acquaintance. Your son's unbelievable." Then he grabbed William's hand. "I hear you put in some mileage in Vietnam. What outfit were you in?"

"101st Airborne Division."

"Good outfit. I also hear you played some hockey."

William glowed. "Yeah. I was almost there, except the war took away my eyes."

The Coach saw the anguish permeating the man's face. So did Ada. "Just think, you're going to be able to do it all over again. And this time, be there. That son of yours is a natural." The Coach saw Eddie and Tommy standing nearby and added, "Those other two boys - they're the best pupils I have." The Coach cheered up everybody that day.

Mary listened to everything. She turned to invite him to join them for pizza, but the man had already left, as silently as a cat.

William decided to have some fun ribbing his mother. "Well, Miss Ogdensburg, what do you have going with the Coach?"

Ada giggled. "Well, he may not know enough to stop drinking, but he does appreciate a good woman when he sees one."

William told Ed at school about the exhilaration he felt at the ice rink, even though he couldn't see the kids skate. Ed became a bit jealous

The next week June called Ada and told her she'd take the boys, Ed wanted to see what an ice rink was all about. The rink was not only a place for the boys to learn hockey, it was also the gathering place for the adults to socialize. By this time, Ada knew all the ins and outs of the hockey parents. June was struck by everyone referring to Ada as Miss Ogdensburg. For the first time, June saw the mean Coach. Everything said about him was true. Now she knew why her boys were tired after the clinic. Even though she didn't know that much about hockey, she saw they were skating like professionals. Ed remarked to William, "The man does yell a lot, doesn't he."

57

William bragged. "He's not so bad. In my day, coaches were a lot tougher." Yet William was worried about the welfare of his son.

When the session was over, Ada and the boys' parents were waiting in the lobby. Ada called out, "Yoo hoo, Coach."

The Coach came over and Ada introduced him to June and Ed. As they shook hands, June felt shivers go down her spine. The Coach, in a voice hoarse from the practice, praised Eddie and Tommy. The Coach said to Ed there were just players and then there were leaders. His sons were leaders. The Coach continued, "I see you're wearing a military jacket. Were you in the service?"

"Well, don't I look like an old leatherneck?"

"Yeah, you do," the Coach answered with a gentle smile. "Vietnam, right?"

The boys were standing around listening to the adults' conversation. The Coach turned to them and in his gruff voice said, "You boys should be as proud as anyone. These are real men I'm standing next to."

Ed asked, "How's little Victor doing?"

Once again the Coach said, "He's a natural."

Mary and William's chests popped out.

The Coach looked at Ada, "But it's the water from Ogdensburg, right ma'am?"

Ada replied, "Sometimes I think you drank the same water."

The expression on the Coach's face changed. Without a sound, he disappeared from the group as the adults were laughing about the inside joke between the Coach and Ada.

Then June spoke, "I know you can't see his eyes, Mary, but they look evil. He may be a good hockey coach, but he gives me the creeps."

"You know I can hear anybody. I know everyone's distinctive walk, but if it weren't for the smell of alcohol on the Coach, I'd never be able to know when he was approaching."

William and Ed agreed with Mary. The man was as silent as a cat.

Ed said, "Just think, you don't have to spend any money going to a bar. Just inhale his breath, you'll get a free drunk."

They left the rink laughing.

By taking the boys to the rink the last few months, Ada had given June and Ed, as well as Mary and William, time to be together. Now it changed. Everybody wanted to go to the rink. William also started wearing his army jacket. The hatred and resentment William harbored towards the government for the loss of his sight was replaced by a pride of having served his country. Little Victor was proud of his father wearing that jacket.

Everyone's life was revolving around the rink. When Ada was shopping in the Loop, she brought a Super 8 movie camera to capture her grandsons' skating. She reasoned that even though Ed, William, and Mary couldn't see their sons, the boys might want to someday look back at their early years. Ada also thought Victor would watch himself to spot his mistakes, but after he saw himself and the novelty wore off, he went back to his playing. Mary and William realized Ada was wonderful to have thought of it.

But for all the good times, there were some hard times. The other kids started making cruel remarks about the blind. Eddie was involved in a couple fights in the locker room. Even Victor's feelings were hurt. One time, the Coach's son Victor started beating an older big mouth: he was just like his father, there was no such thing as mercy. His father walked into the locker room and saw the fight. The Coach took no sides, he simply asked, "What's going on?"

Since neither boy would say, Tommy spoke up and explained that the boy was making fun of blind people.

The Coach looked at the boys and told them, "Little Victor's father may be blind, but he's a hero. He was also one hockey player who could have made it to the pros. If you can grow up and achieve any of what Victor's father has done, or Eddie and Tommy's father, you'd have the right then to shoot off your mouth. But otherwise keep you mouth shut."

The Coach turned and walked out of the locker room. The silence was deafening. Then the boy said to Victor, "I'm sorry. That was stupid of me. I didn't really mean it."

After that problem was solved, the Coach's son Victor asked little Victor if he wanted to see him figure skate. The two boys, although a year apart in age, were becoming close friends. Little Victor said, "Victor, it gets really confusing with both of us having the same name. Can I call you what your Dad calls you?"

"Yeah, sure, you can call me Moe."

After the practice, Victor asked Grandma Ada if she could bring him back later so he could watch Moe figure skate. For the first time, Grandma raised her voice and said, "No!"

Mary and William had heard the request and understood the reason for Ada's refusal.

"Miss Ogdensburg," William spoke, "I see no problem with bringing Victor back to see his friend skate."

Ada was relieved to hear William's approval. She didn't want her son or his family to be upset, yet she never wanted to disappoint her grandson. She leaned down to Victor and whispered, "I think that will be exciting."

Victor grinned from ear to ear.

Later in the afternoon, Ada brought Victor back to the rink. This time she got to sit in the bleachers next to her grandson and catch his enthusiasm as they watched the figure skating class. Ada was enchanted by the girls in their cute little outfits and was secretly wishing that Mary and William would have a little girl. She also watched Moe, and just as in hockey, the boy was far ahead of the other skaters. He was leaping in the air, but showed a gracefulness she'd never seen from him before.

"Grandma, did you see how Moe jumped?"

"I think he's great. His father really spends a lot of time with him,"

A woman sitting on the bleacher below turned upward to Ada and said, "He gets his skating from my side of the family. His father may spend time with him, but only if it's pertaining to sports. Otherwise he's in the bars getting drunk or playing with his life. I couldn't take it anymore. That's why we're divorced."

Ada replied, "Moe's your son? He's fantastic. This is Victor, he's one of Moe's hockey friends. Moe invited us to watch him skate."

The woman icily responded, "His name is Victor. Moe is the nickname his father gave him."

Ada introduced herself and Victor to the Coach's ex-wife, Dorothy.

Dorothy acknowledged Ada. "Oh, your son is one of the blind parents. I've heard about you. Your son was wounded in the war, but it seems that your son adjusted to life. Not everyone has."

Victor was ignoring the women's conversation, he was staring at the figure skaters. "Grandma, look at Moe jump again. Look at those crossovers."

Victor's mother continued, "It's not his father that's made him a figure skater. It's these classes. Even the pro hockey teams have instructors who teach them basic crossovers and edges and power skating."

This was Greek to Ada, but she was memorizing every word Dorothy said. The rest of the session went quietly, Ada and Victor were watching Moe's every move.

When the session ended, Victor met Moe in the lobby. The boys excitedly talked about Moe's class. Moe asked Victor, "Well, do you think you parents will let you sign up?"

"I don't know. I don't think my Grandma likes figure skating and she's the one who brings me."

When Ada and Victor were home, Victor couldn't stop talking about Moe's figure skating. Ada couldn't stand it anymore and retreated to her bedroom. Victor kept chattering. William knew something was wrong. He went into Ada's room to discuss it.

Ada wept. "William, you know I love Victor, Mary, and you with all my heart. I would do anything I could for my family. But it hurts me to hear Victor raving about figure skating, knowing the pain you've gone through because of it. Now I'm going to be the bad guy because I have to protect you from any more hurt."

Mary was listening and heard William laughing. "Oh Mom, I love you so much. But I guess you didn't realize that I've been able to put Elizabeth into the past. That was another time and place. I've come to accept this path in life. I could never have

61

been as happy as I am now. You, Mary, and Victor have replaced the bitterness and anger with love. It won't bother me at all if Victor wants to try figure skating. I'm just worried about you having to do so much and never having time for yourself."

William hugged Ada as she dried her tears. Ada called Mary into the bedroom. Ada felt better, but she wouldn't feel totally satisfied until she told them her news. "I've got to tell you what I found out. The Coach was married. We sat right behind his ex-wife. Let me tell you, she loves her son and dotes on him. But when it comes to her former husband, she's very bitter. You know we've all seen Moe's skating ability and we know it comes from his father. But this woman has the audacity to claim it's because of her providing the proper figure skating lessons. Imagine that! William, is it true that professional hockey teams use figure skating to improve their players?"

William nodded.

"Well, Dorothy said they do. Perhaps we should enroll Victor so his hockey can improve. He might even out-skate Moe."

After that discussion, Ada was on the phone telling Sr. Richard the same story.

That night in bed, Mary rolled over to William. "You are happy, aren't you? I heard your mother talk about that girl Elizabeth. You once told me about her. If you wouldn't have lost your sight, and there was a choice between Elizabeth and me, who would you have chosen?"

"The woman with class. Do I have to say anymore?" And he gave her a peck on her cheek.

Mary went to sleep smiling with self-confidence.

The next day at the Lighthouse, William told Ed about Victor joining the figure skating class.

Ed replied, "Only queers and three-legged steers wear those outfits."

William was so angry that he gave Ed the cold shoulder the rest of the day.

Ed knew William was upset, so on the way home Ed admitted, "Maybe that will make Victor a better skater."

Their friendship returned to normal.

Victor and Moe became inseparable. When Moe came to Victor's house, Ada gently probed him for details about his father. Moe ended it by saying, "I don't know that much about my father. I only know he was an athlete."

Another time, William and Mary were over at June and Ed's house while Grandma was watching Victor and Moe. Ada laid down for a little nap while the boys occupied themselves. They were trying to make sling shots and they needed rubber bands. Victor remembered seeing some around the cans in the pantry. Little did he know those rubber bands told Mary the contents of the cans: one rubber band for peas, two for corn, and so on. The boys took every one in sight. Sling shots in hand, they turned the living room into a battlefield. The furniture was overturned and repositioned into fortresses.

William and Mary came home and walked into a war zone. The boys were so engrossed in their game, they never heard the door open. William and Mary tripped over the chair. Then Ada heard the noise and came out to see them on the floor with the boys hovering over them. Victor then realized why Grandma had told him time and again to keep things in their place.

Mary and William knew there hadn't been a tornado. The boys quickly explained and apologized as they helped the parents off the floor.

William said, "I guess you boys should be furniture movers."

Mary remarked, "Just feel these rugs. I've never been this close to them. I guess I have some vacuuming to do."

Ada supervised the boys as they straightened the living room while Mary went to prepare them their favorite supper: hot dogs, potato chips, and pork and beans.

While sitting at the table, Mary heard the boys giggling and whispering. She assumed they were just being silly.

William put a spoonful of pork and beans into his mouth and wondered if Mary had lost her chef's touch. It tasted like hot fruit cocktail. What was going on?

The boys were nearly in hysterics. Finally Mary asked, "What's so funny?"

Victor gasped, "Mom, you cooked the fruit cocktail!"

"No, I didn't - that's pork and beans. Quit being like your Uncle Ed."

Ada entered the kitchen and looked at the plates, suppressing a giggle. "Boys, did you move the cans and take off the rubber bands?"

Victor admitted it. "Yes, Grandma. We needed the rubber bands for our sling shots."

Ada rebuked them. "You know what I told you about moving things."

Mary joined the laughter. Grandma warmed up some real pork and beans. Moe received his first peek into the world of the sightless.

For the next few years, life was beautiful. Victor was enrolled at St. Benedict Grade School. Ada took him to school and picked him up each day. He continued with hockey and figure skating. Victor was catching up to Moe in figure skating, but Moe with a personality like his father's had an inner drive that made him a better hockey player.

The Coach remained the same - he only spoke when he wanted. He increased his alcoholic consumption, but he still got the job done. He was asked to coach a squirt team at McFetridge, a newly built rink in Chicago. It seemed that the Coach was the breeding ground for this new arena: every boy in the clinic left Rainbo and won positions on the elite McFetridge traveling teams, even Tommy and Eddie. The Coach remained loyal and taught the hockey clinic at Rainbo every Sunday. It was amazing that McFetridge had winning teams from its inception: the suburban teams were envious, little did they know McFetridge had gotten its raw material from Rainbo and the Coach fashioned them into winning athletes. His squirt team was the cream of the crop - he had a fantastic center, his own son and a left winger, Victor who was faster than a streak of lightning.

William and Mary went to every game. Although they couldn't see, they heard the man on the mike announce Victor LaBuld scoring or assisting. Moe was the top scorer, but he also amassed the most penalty minutes. Moe always was one step up on Victor because they both were competing in figure skating. They were best friends and the competition between them cemented their friendship.

Ada tried to get to know Dorothy better and she realized Dorothy didn't really know what her former husband was all about. Dorothy constantly told her, "He's such a waste."

Ada got to know some of the other parents in figure skating. She found there was a considerable amount of jealousy and politics in the sport. One was trying to outdo the other with expensive outfits. The figure skating teacher was offered bribes for extra considerations. Other parents would tell Ada what a marvelous skater Victor was. Yet those same parents would scream at their own children, "You can beat him."

The most disliked boy was Moe: he was too good. If Dorothy had learned anything from the Coach, it was to watch how people reveal their true colors. She remained aloof from them. If she had anything to say it would have been told only to Ada.

In the competition at the end of the year, all the figure skaters were dressed in their sequined costumes. Parents, grandparents, relatives and friends were there. June warned Ed to watch his remarks about figure skaters.

Mary in her new dress, also cautioned Ed. The other parents glared at them: blind people had no business at a competition. Even the Coach dressed in a suit was there. As he walked in, heads turned. He greeted Ada and her extended family, but as soon as he saw his ex-wife, disappeared into the crowd. When the performances began, the parents in the audience held their breath hoping their child would be perfect to win the trophy.

Moe came out on the ice dressed as Uncle Sam, from his skates to his top hat. His routine was outstanding. He did waltz jumps which his age group didn't even try to do. If he had one flaw it was his powerful legs with a stance too wide for a figure skater. At the conclusion, he received a great round of applause, the parents knew no one could ever beat him.

The announcer introduced Victor LaBuld. The whispers circulated in the bleachers, "That's the boy with the blind parents."

The music started. Victor went into his act. His spirals and crossovers were superb. His black tux emphasized every graceful move.

Mary kept asking, "How's he doing?"

The reply was, "He's fantastic."

William and Ed weren't really into it. They came hoping the Coach would be there to shoot the breeze with them. Eddie and Tommy admired their adopted brother. He was quieting the crowd as he skated. At the end of his performance, there was a new threat: Victor received a standing ovation.

The trophies were announced, "First place is awarded to Victor Wolf." William and Ed were still engrossed in their conversation, even when Victor LaBuld was announced as the second place winner. The crowd was again on its feet applauding. Mary nudged William, "That's your son these people are applauding. Will you start paying attention."

After the other trophies were given out and the show was over, the people began their malarkey. "Your son should have won. He was marvelous." William finally took notice of his son.

As both boys walked to the lobby, no one saw or heard Moe apologizing to Victor, "You were better than me. I only do this to make my Mother happy. I'm really a hockey player. I'm like my Dad."

Victor was hugged by all the ladies in his life. His father also hugged him, but deep within William's heart, he felt figure skating was only a passing fancy, a means to an end, conditioning for a career in hockey.

The Coach walked up to the group, "Victor, you did a great job. You were fantastic. When you go home, pat yourself on the back for a job well done."

These encouraging words pierced William's brain: the Coach felt his son had done something above and beyond the call of duty.

Ed couldn't hold back any longer. "As long as he doesn't give out $3.00 bills."

The Coach's voice changed. "If people only knew the skill of skating, they wouldn't make fun of male figure skaters. I'd rather endure Jump School at Fort Bragg than take the punishment these figure skaters go through."

Ed knew by the Coach's voice that his joke wasn't funny. He changed the subject. "You went through Jump School, Coach?"

"Yeah, they taught us how to jump without parachutes."

Before Mary could say anything to the Coach, he was gone. He had seen Dorothy approaching.

Dorothy's congratulations were sincere. "You did so well, Victor. To be honest with you, I think you should have won."

Ada spoke up about Moe, "Those jumps Victor takes, it would be hard for an older kid to beat him."

Dorothy answered, "He does jump well. But if only people knew that his father takes him out at 5:00 in the morning to run hurdles. Then there's baseball. You name it, Victor has to do it. The only time he gets to be a little boy is when he's with your grandson. All his father sees in Victor is himself again. Eventually I'm going to put my foot down. Victor has to have time to enjoy being a boy."

As Ada was driving her family home, Mary naively asked, "William, what did the Coach mean when he said he jumped from an airplane without a parachute? How could he do that?"

"Oh that's an old Special Forces joke." William went into a deep silence.

Finally, he spoke, "Mom, what is Moe's last name?"

"I think it's Wolf."

William's head started spinning. He was telling himself it was impossible. Then it hit him. The Coach's words echoed in his head, "When you go home..." It was the same voice on the elevator in Buffalo, but his words then were, "I don't want to go home..."

"Oh my God," William grabbed Mary's hand.

"What's wrong, William? Are you hurting or something?"

"I'm afraid."

"What are you afraid of?"

"The bogeyman."

Victor heard this and turned around from the front seat. "You said there's no such thing as a bogeyman."

67

William realized what he had said. He changed the subject by praising Victor's performance.

That night in bed, William explained everything to Mary. "You wonder why you can't hear the Coach walk and why he drinks so much. I heard about him in the hospital in Buffalo. They said he was a butcher capable of killing anything that walked. They cured him physically of his war wounds, but they took away his medals and honor and sent him to prison. Mary, I love my country and I respect any soldier who fought for it. But the group the Coach belonged to were heartless people. Even the regular soldiers were afraid of them. You never knew when they were going to lose it."

"Are you saying we should take Victor out of hockey, or take him somewhere else?"

"I'm saying one of us has to be with Ada at all times at hockey. But don't tell my mother. I don't think little Moe knows about his dad."

A week later, destiny took its course. William didn't have to worry about the Coach: he was in Holy Family Hospital in critical condition because of an accident at work.

The hockey parents were saddened by this news. Little Moe took it the hardest, he withdrew into a shell. Victor and Ada tried to call him many times, but Dorothy apologized and said he wouldn't talk to anyone.

McFetridge picked up a coach to finish the season. Rainbo did the same with an instructor. For the first time, the hockey parents realized the impact the Coach had on their boys.

Ed was upset because he enjoyed reliving his service days. He did appreciate the great job the Coach had been doing with the boys on the ice, but Ed savored the reminiscing.

William sat many nights asking God's forgiveness for not trusting the Coach with his son. He remembered Miss Kay's words pertaining to Victor Wolf: the man had lost his soul. But if he lost his soul, why did he teach those youngsters and give his time to hockey? Was this his way of asking God's forgiveness? Sr. Richard had explained how God forgave everyone.

68

Ada lost a friend - he didn't talk much, but he always recognized her.

Victor continued with figure skating. Moe was no longer there. Victor persisted in calling his friend, but to no avail. Moe was in a deep depression. It became so bad that his mother and he moved to Rolling Meadows.

The summer passed quickly, as quickly as the Coach and his son had come into Victor's life, they were gone. Victor's life was like a book with a missing chapter, no one would ever know the complete story.

Ada kept Victor occupied: private figure skating lessons at Skokie because Rainbo closed for the summer and McFetridge didn't have any professionals to teach figure skating. Victor rarely mentioned Moe, had he forgotten the memory of Moe or was it too painful to remember his best friend?

Victor poured all his energies into figure skating. He was learning to jump. Every so often he'd ask Ada, "Do you think Moe would think I'm doing good?"

Ada's reply was always, "He would have put out his hand and said, 'Give me five!' "

At the Skokie rink, an athletic woman constantly watched Victor. Finally one week, she walked up to Ada, "Hi, my name is Evelyn Rubin. I'm a figure skating instructor. I'd like to be blunt with you. Your grandson out there has the potential to be a winner. I was a silver medalist in the Olympics for Canada. But gold sparkles all around him."

Ada took a deep breath. This woman was serious! Ada had always seen the fun side of figure skating. Did her grandson have a chance to be a contender?

Miss Rubin gave Ada her card and told her to think it over and let her know by September.

That evening Ada discussed it with William and Mary. For a while William dreamed of his son at the Olympics. But reality set in. William's overriding concern had always been hockey. He knew a skater couldn't excel in both.

When hockey started in the fall, Victor wasn't the same. The new coach at McFetridge didn't really know the underlying spirit of hockey or the little men he was dealing with. He was a lot nicer than Coach Wolf. He fraternized with the parents - he was out to make hockey a fun game.

Victor outshined everyone at those early practices, but the espirit de corps was gone. It was apparent when Victor wouldn't go to the practices. Finally Ada had to tell William the spark had died.

William tried to ignite Victor's enthusiasm. He explained that Grandma, Mom, and himself had invested a lot of time, energy, and money in hockey. It wasn't fair of Victor to let everyone down.

Victor broke into tears. He sobbed, "It hurts when I go out on the ice. The Coach's breath isn't there. We don't have a reason for getting mean. I miss my best friend. It's not the same without him. The only time I feel good on the ice is when I do my jumps. Moe knew I could do them. He wants me to be better than him. I really don't want to play hockey anymore."

William angrily shook Victor. "For nine years it's been everything to make you happy - but what about what I want, what I need?"

Mary and Ada were upset by everything they'd heard. They came to Victor's rescue. Mary screamed, "Leave him alone." Ada knew better than to get into it. Mary said, "Ada, take Victor outside."

Mary lashed into William, "Are you trying to destroy our son? Is this fucking hockey so great that it's more important than your son? You men are all alike. Do you have to relive your life through your son? Or is it the glory you need to recapture? Do you know what glory really is, William? Glory is raising a child the best you can. Shielding and protecting him from pain, but giving him the independence to be himself. Victor has a problem now and it could get worse. He's lost his best friend. Can't you understand that? I did not like the Coach at first, he was creepy to me. But I learned to respect him because he gave my son his own personality. If you weren't talking to Ed in the bleachers, you would have heard the Coach say, 'Be yourself. Don't try to imitate other people.' What are you doing to Victor? Are you letting him have his own personality? Do you feel the hurt he's feeling now? I don't want to hear how you lost your eyes in a war. God blessed you by giving you a healthy son. You will live on just by him carrying your name. To me, that's enough."

Mary turned around to join Ada and Victor. The tears were still in Victor's eyes, as well as Ada's. All three wept.

William sat in his chair and thought. For the first time his wife was angry with him. She'd never talked like this before. He was about to damn God until he realized how true Mary's words were. He must be thankful just to have a healthy son. Then he thought of the Coach: he only played professional hockey a short time, why? God must have his reasons. But William knew God had given him two angels to be his negotiators, and Mary and Ada would not let him stray too far off course.

William understood how deeply he'd hurt his son and family. He got up from his chair and joined them on the porch. "You know, I'm hungry. Ada, get the car. I think we'll eat out tonight."

Victor grabbed his Dad's hand. "I'll try to be a better hockey player, Dad."

"Who gives a shit about hockey? I'm more concerned about you winning a gold medal in figure skating."

"I'm not that good, Dad."

"But you'll try. Won't you? Then Moe will be proud of you. All of us will be proud of you."

By those words Mary knew that although William's heart may have been hurt, his love for his son would heal the wounds.

When they got in the car Ada saw everything was alright. They drove the short distance to a restaurant on Lincoln Avenue near Damen and Irving Park aptly named The Lincoln Restaurant. The owners, John and Loula Athans, saw them approaching and accommodated them. Ada thanked them for their kindness. Loula explained that they were used to helping people with vision problems. The Lions Club held their weekly meetings at the restaurant. There was also a group of blind bowlers who came in after their weekly games at the bowling alley across the street.

71

"Bowlers?" William was astounded.

"Oh yes. They bowl just like anyone else. Are you interested in joining them?"

William said yes - for a couple reasons: one, to see if it could really be done and two, to let his son see he could try new things and change.

Then Ada mentioned, "What about your buddy?"

"You know, this is a way I can kick his ass."

Mary spoke gently, "Maybe it will be reversed." She was still angry at her husband.

That evening in bed, William rolled over and held Mary's hand. "You know I have a complaint about you. When I married you, I thought you were so innocent that you could have been the sister of the Blessed Mother. Today I found out that your language leaves a lot to be desired. You swore at me. But you know what, I would have sworn at me, too. You made me recognize what I was doing to our son. You also made me realize how much God has blessed us. But you know, I'm going to kick Ed's ass in bowling."

Mary spoke, "Do you realize what you're saying?"

"Yeah, I'm going to kick Ed's ass."

"Why?"

"Because he's my friend."

"Now you know how your son feels about Moe. As much as you love Ed, Victor loves Moe."

Mary went to sleep with the satisfied smile of a psychiatrist.

CHAPTER FIVE

At the Lighthouse William mentioned the blind bowling team he was going to join. He anticipated Ed would ask to also learn to bowl. Before you knew it, William and Ed were becoming pros. Their teammates enjoyed Ed's sense of humor and became immune to William's incessant descriptions of his son the figure skater. Mary encouraged her husband in his new sport, it gave her more time with her son.

Ada contacted Miss Rubin and Victor was on his way. Ada thought Evelyn was tough - she seemed to have come from the same mold as Coach Wolf. Victor loved it. Mary and William asked Ada about every session. Ada related how unbelievable he was and that Miss Rubin was pleased. In his heart, William still felt the loss of hockey.

After each bowling session, the team stopped for drinks and a snack at the Lincoln Restaurant. Ed and William allowed one special teammate, Ian, into their world. As she served them their drinks, Jewel the bartender stood in amazement at how blind people could be so active in life. One of the funniest episodes occurred when Ed asked Ian how well he knew the Bible.

Ian answered, "I know it inside and out."

"If you know it that well, then tell me who was the first carpenter?"

"Well, let me see. I guess it could be Noah, he did make a pretty big boat."

"No. Eve. She made Adam's banana stand!"

Ed had them all laughing and couldn't stop now, he was on a roll. He continued, "I can prove Adam wasn't black."

In his Boston accent Ian asked, "How can you prove that?"

"Did you ever take a rib from a black?"

The groans of laughter went on for another hour. Ed tried to outdo himself.

A drunk at the end of the bar wouldn't let go of the black joke. Even though it was the bowlers' party, the man got off his stool and staggered to them. He spouted racial remarks about the blacks in Chicago and the rest of the country. The blind men tried to ignore him, but his foreign accent imposed itself rudely on them. He persisted that blacks never fought for America.

Ed had reached his fill and told him off, "Listen you d.p. son of a bitch. You'd better go to one of our libraries and read how many black heroes came out of America. You'd better see how many died in Vietnam and not just there but every war. Did you fight for this country? No. You come to this country to eat off the American table. But it was the black soldier who helped set that table and you foreigners come over here and want to take over the whole banquet."

Jewel saw things were escalating so she asked the drunk to leave. The night continued until Ed slyly got Jewel aside and gave her a $10.00 tip. She told him he didn't have to do that. But he insisted, "You got that pain in the ass away from us. I appreciate that."

"I didn't want to see your friend get hurt."

"William doesn't bruise that easily."

"No, I mean your other friend, the black man."

"You mean Ian? He's not black. He's from Boston."

"Well, you'd better take another look." Then she realized what she said. "Maybe you'd better ask him."

Now Ed felt embarrassed at having told black jokes. He returned to his friend. "Ian, I want to apologize to you. I didn't know you were a black. Those jokes were out of line." William stood still listening and thinking to himself, "Ian's a black?"

Ian replied, "There's no problem. Your jokes were funny. I can laugh at a good joke and if it pokes fun at my people, I can appreciate it when I know you're not ridiculing us because you're prejudiced. Some people get real upset, but those individuals aren't at peace with themselves. You've got to accept yourself and your limitations. I can laugh just as hard at a blind joke because I've accepted who I am. Look at you. Because I speak with a Boston accent you didn't know I was black. We're friends. Maybe God should take all the prejudiced people and make them blind. They'll never know there are other colors in a box of crayons. To them, it's just a box of crayons.

To me it's the rainbow of life. Ed, I thank you for sticking up for my people and my country."

William remained silent.   Then Ian lightened up the atmosphere by telling jokes. Jewel listened, laughing to herself how these men didn't know their friend was black.

This night would be memorable for everyone.

It was nearly closing time, so Jewel called a cab for Ian, William, and Ed. All three were intoxicated. They first dropped off Ian, then Ed. At William's house, he couldn't fit the key into the keyhole. Mary let him in. She went back to bed angry that another night's sleep had been disturbed by drunkenness. William had to go to the bathroom. He had lost all sense of direction. He went into Ada's room and urinated in her lingerie drawer. Ada woke up to see her son fumbling and mumbling, "Where's the handle?"

She screamed at him, "William, go to bed."

"But Mom, you always tell me I have to be a big boy and flush the toilet."

"William, just go to bed."

In the morning, Ada awakened to find all her underwear thoroughly soaked. This was the last straw. She finally spoke to her son about his drinking. Mary backed her up.

"You're acting like a drunken sailor."

William's bloodshot eyes looked at his mother. "I wasn't in the navy. I was in the army."

Ada told him what he had done to her underwear. William was mortified. Mary couldn't contain herself any longer and burst into hysterics.

William went to the Lighthouse hungover and humiliated. Ed and William commiserated about how their wives bitched at them for being drunk. They also discussed their buddy Ian.

In the Vocational Training room, Ed was busy working on a deck of cards. He was inventing a new playing method. With the instructor's help, he poked each card with a darning needle so blind people could feel the suit and numbers.

When they'd finished, Ed got some sandpaper to sand certain edges on the cards to let only him know the aces and face cards. This was a little trick he'd picked up in the service. The instructor got the picture of what Ed was up to. He chuckled to himself, "That cheat." Finally he said, "Ed, you're many things, but I never thought of you as a card shark."

"Why do you say that?"

"I know why you're sanding those cards."

Ed gave him a shrug. "I was dealt a bad hand in life. I lost my eyes. Now I'm going to control the deck. Don't you think that's fair? I want you to promise to tell no one, especially my buddy William."

The instructor gave his word and kept it.

At Ed's house a new weekly activity began: card playing. The key players were Mel, Ian, William, and any sucker Ed could find.

First Ed explained his marking system to his two buddies, conveniently neglecting to mention the sanded areas. They were enthusiastic and grateful that Ed was ingenious enough to devise a marking system so they could gamble. Mel was enjoying himself, he felt he had the advantage because of his sight and he could improve from an excellent poker player to a superior one. Ian was at a slight disadvantage, having never played before.

When they got down to the nitty gritty of the game, week after week Ed was the big winner. Ian may have been the best bowler, but Ed was the luckiest at cards.

The wives were relieved that their husbands were at home instead of a bar. June could effectively control the amount of drinking. Ian's sister, Willis, was his chauffeur. Finally one week, she accepted June's invitation to wait with them for the card game to end. Now the ladies met in the living room while the men congregated in the basement rec room. The ladies were enchanted by the new edition to their group. Willis told them how grateful she was that Ian had met Ed and William. Before he had only his bowling. Now all he talked about was Ed did this, Ed said that. Their friendship had given Ian another dimension to his life. Ian lived with Willis and her husband John, a Town Hall District policeman. Willis explained that whenever John was on duty, he patrolled near the bowling alley to keep an eye on Ian and his friends.

June emotionally responded by hugging Willis. "I'm always so worried about those knuckleheads whenever they go out. I'm glad you told us about this guardian angel."

As the weeks went by, Ed was accumulating large amounts of money in his jar. No one complained that Ed was winning. They wished some luck would rub off on them.

The cards were wearing out, so Ian sent Willis out to buy a couple new decks. He called June to ask her to bring over the old deck so he could faithfully duplicate Ed's system.

When John saw and felt the first card, he knew something wasn't right. As he went through the deck, he discovered some cards were marked. He mentioned it to Ian. Ian replied, "Of course, how else do you think three blind men could play?"

"No - I don't mean marked legally. I mean secretly marked. Here, feel the corner. It's been sanded."

"I don't believe it. Are you sure?"

"Yeah, remember, I deal with criminals and cheats every day."

Ian leaned back in his chair. A grin covered his face.

"That son of a bitch."

"Are you sure this man's your friend?"

Angrily Ian fumed, "He's my best friend. He not only does it to me, he also does it to his other good friend and his brother-in-law. He may be despicable, but he'd give me the shirt off his back. But I need your help to get even. Do you know how to mark cards like that?"

"No, I just know how to read them. But I know some people who do."

"When we're done punching these holes, can you give them to your people and have them marked using my secret system?"

John smiled, "You're just as despicable!"

That evening while on duty, John stopped in to see one of his jailbirds. When John told him he was there to get two decks of cards marked, the man was relieved. When he'd finished, the jailbird explained that he had done such a great job on the cards, that only a surgeon or blind man could feel the markings.

John said, "I know just the person."

The next day John taught Ian how to read the marked cards. Willis observed from the kitchen her husband and brother.

That evening she asked her husband, "What are you doing with Ian and those cards?"

John looked at his wife and couldn't stop laughing.

She stomped her foot, "What's so funny?"

"Your brother is a cheat. I should lock him up and throw away the key."

Willis was indignant. "My brother has never cheated in his life. You have no right to insult his honor."

After John told her the story and what was going to happen, Willis should have taken a life preserver to bed with her because the tears of laughter were flooding the bed.

When Willis returned the decks to June, she had to tell her what was going on.

June exclaimed, "That son of a bitch. He'd cheat his own friends! We've got to watch this."

The next card game, everyone was there. Ed sat at the table with a smile of confidence. William and Mel hoped they'd have a little luck to beat Ed. Ian - cool, calm, and collected - sat there like a lawyer who had the trial prearranged.

Ian was the dealer and he chose to play Black Jack. Ed was known to bluff successfully. As long as Ian dealt the cards, Ed's losses mounted. There was no way Ed could beat the house.

Finally Ed dealt the cards and felt he should have been the big winner. But as luck would have it, Ian won.

Ed couldn't understand it. He called up to June, "Have the kids been messing with the cards?"

"Why, dear, is there something wrong?"

"They just don't feel right."

June couldn't contain herself any longer. "You cheat. You know, Ed, you have done some raunchy things. But to cheat your friends! How does the shoe feel when it's on the other foot?" She added, "I'm sorry, Ian."

"Why are you telling him you're sorry?"

Ian spoke up, "These are my cards - "

Ed became uncharacteristically silent. Finally he sheepishly said, "Oh you must have put the holes in the wrong spots."

"No, the holes are in the right spots, it's just that the sanding's a little different."

June's smile crossed her face from ear to ear. "How low can you stoop, Ed? You cheated your own friends."

Mel and William got the picture. As they came down on Ed, he finally told them, "I wasn't cheating you. This has been a fund raiser for the enterprise we're going into."

"What enterprise is this?" William asked sarcastically.

"We're going to open up a newspaper stand. And Ian is going to be the gourmet chef of the hot dog cart."

"You can't get out of this one, Ed," said William.

"No, it's true. I'll show you. June, go up to the bedroom and get the big jar full of money."

When June returned with it, William read aloud the Braille label, "Four Blind Mice, Inc." They knew Ed was telling the truth.

William asked him, "Why do you say "Four Blind Mice? Mel's not blind."

Ed came back, "He's got a pair of eyes, but he couldn't spot a cheat. You can't get much blinder than that."

Mel had to laugh at himself. The card game was put on the back burner for the rest of the night. The men concentrated on the enterprise. Mel totally immersed himself in the project, just like the card games and everything the blind men did. He loved his brother-in-law and his friends. Even though Mel wasn't a soldier who sacrificed his eyes, he gave back to his country by helping these men who had.

At his law office, Mel did the telephoning and paper work to get the licenses and legal papers completed. He bought the hot dog cart and had a carpenter build the newspaper stand on the corner of Damen and Roscoe. After a month the Four Blind Mice were in business.

It was a bittersweet scene when William and Ed had to tell their friends and instructors at the Lighthouse that they were leaving to start their new venture. The school personnel felt the pang of separation knowing they had given the men the skills and confidence to tackle the new endeavor, while grasping that their loss was the men's gain.

Ian, being a good cook, knew he had to serve the best hot dogs in Chicago, so he served Vienna hot dogs which Mel bought directly from the factory at Damen and Elston.

The men had devised the work schedules so nothing interfered with their Tuesday night bowling. Ada drove William to the paper stand at 5:00 A.M. At first it was difficult for him. With Ada's help he got himself into the routine and eventually did it by himself. William wanted the early shift so he could be home with Mary at the end of her day at the hospital.

Willis and June shared the morning driving chores. Willis's van easily held the hot dog cart. Willis and Ian picked up Ed about 10:30 each morning or June would drive him to the Reed house. In the evening about 10:00 Willis, or John if he was off duty, picked up Ed, Ian, and the cart.

Many guardian angels were watching. Ian's brother-in-law provided the security. John told his fellow officers to patrol the newsstand and keep a sharp eye out. On her way to the store, June would drive by and blow her husband a kiss. Willis also drove by and saw how her brother had allowed himself to leave his island of loneliness and enter a world of friendship. She had always felt a sense of guilt that she could see and her brother couldn't. She was her brother's keeper.

Little Eddie was no longer little, the nineteen year old was going to college for criminal justice so he'd have an advantage when he applied to the Chicago Police Department. Eddie helped run the stand on Tuesday nights so his Dad could bowl.

They say people are only as old as they feel, but that wasn't Ada's case. Between the paper stand and Victor's skating, Ada had found a fountain of youth. When she wasn't on the run, she took time out at the Lincoln Restaurant where she had become one of the regulars. The only group she couldn't get close to were the figure skating parents, they were too uppity and jealous. Victor was a shining star on the ice, an aura of fascination and enchantment surrounded him. Everyone stopped to watch him.

He won all his competitions which didn't surprise Miss Rubin. She was a professional and knew what the others didn't.

At one competition which Victor's entire extended family including Willis and Ian attended, the figure skating parents stared at the blind adults - it never changed. Willis was amazed at Victor's grace and agility. She kept grabbing Mary's shoulder, telling her how beautiful Victor looked and how she and William had to be proud of him. William overheard her; he was proud of his son, but still in the back of his mind knew the boy could have been just as good a hockey player.

Ed sat next to a woman cradling a small infant. Ed had eaten too many of Ian's hot peppers and his stomach was bloated with gas. He had more gas than the entire state of Texas. Armed with a silencer, Ed cut loose some of the gas. Everyone stared incredulously - trying to appear innocent and implicate someone else. Ed could hear the whispers and feel the stares. He turned to the woman and coyly said, "Ma'am, I think you need to change your baby's diapers." The rest of the audience stared as the embarrassed woman left. The distraction was short lived. The people quickly returned to watching Victor's performance.

After every contest Victor gave the trophy to his mom and hugged his dad. As Victor was being congratulated this day, a man and his daughter walked up to Victor and gave him the typical spiel of what a great job he had done on the ice. He added a new twist: he offered to sponsor the boy if he'd skate with his daughter, Sherri.

Miss Rubin walked by to hear Victor answer, "I have only one coach and I do what Miss Rubin says."

Leonard Winters replied, "I'll get Miss Rubin to train the both of you."

Victor's family listened in stunned silence.

Mr. Winters was introduced to Miss Rubin and offered her a proposition she couldn't refuse. She knew it would bring more ice time and glory to Victor. Before she agreed to anything, she asked Ada if it was alright.

Ada answered, "I don't have any say-so. It's up to Victor's parents."

William and Mary were proud to be recognized as Victor's parents and have someone sponsor their son.

Mary asked Ada, "Would this be too much driving for you?"

"No, I want to help out in any way I can."

The matter was then settled.

As the group left the rink, Ed warned William, "This man sounds like a con artist. Be careful of what you're letting yourself into. It sounds like he wants to take advantage of Victor's talent and fame."

"How can you call him a con artist? He's going to pay for everything. The only con artist I know is you, you card shark." But William should have marked Ed's words.

Months later, Victor and Sherri were ready for their first performance. Once again, Miss Rubin had done her job well. Victor made Sherri look like a diamond. Winning was always in the bag.

Mr. Winters treated Victor as though he were royalty. He bought everything the boy needed or wanted, from custom made skates to expensive costumes. His chauffeur went to the LaBuld house to pick up Victor for each session. Victor enjoyed traveling to other states for competitions. Mr. Winters doted upon Victor as if he were his own son.

But Mr. Winters seldom talked to the rest of Victor's family. He felt it was beneath his dignity to deal with blind people who worked in menial occupations. He insulated himself from anyone less than perfect. He also let everyone know that the trophies were the result of his daughter's talent: Victor was a good skater, but his daughter was the real star.

Miss Rubin started to understand what was going on. Because of their successes, the daughter was being cast in her father's image. Victor remained the same, an athlete who loved the skating and music more than the trophy itself. He would always shake hands with the competitors and sincerely compliment them on their routine. He constantly searched the bleachers - not for his parents or coach, but hoping to see his lost friend to win his approval. Mr. Winters and his crowd relished the limelight. Victor's family quietly accepted his natural abilities.

Following one competition, Mr. Winters was passing out invitations to the figure skating parents to a victory party at his Highland Park estate. Ada and Victor were invited. As they looked at the card, Ada finally grasped what Mr. Winters was all about. William and Mary's names were missing.

Indignation flowed through Ada's veins. She approached Mr. Winters. "You made a mistake on this card. Victor's parents aren't invited."

Mr. Winters was partially intoxicated and mumbled, "I didn't think they'd be able to make the trip." And then muttered under his breath, "I have too many valuable antiques and I don't want them breaking anything in my home."

It didn't take an adult to realize the contempt Mr. Winters harbored. Victor's brain registered it instantly, "I don't really want to go to your dumb old party. And I don't want to skate with your daughter. Her crossovers suck. I don't need a skating partner who drags me down. Besides that my father's a hero and so is my Uncle Ed. You know what? I'm just like my Dad. I don't want to be around pussies. Let's go, Grandma."

Mr. Winters tried to placate them. "Oh Victor, you don't mean that. Your parents are welcomed to my house any time."

Victor and Ada kept walking until they spotted Miss Rubin. Victor said, "I'm not skating anymore in pairs. If you don't want to teach me anymore as an individual, that's okay."

Miss Rubin looked at Victor, then Ada. Smiling, she agreed, "It's about time you understand what's been going on. Victor, it's you I'm interested in. It's you who's going to win for me. All Mr. Winters's money cannot buy me or the glory of knowing that I've trained the best. And you are the best. Now give me five." And she put out her hand.

Ada smiled.

Victor contradicted her, "I'm not really the best. My friend Victor Wolf was the best."

Miss Rubin nodded. In the back of her mind she remembered the sparkle from that star.

Victor and Ada walked to Mary, William and their other guests. Victor announced, "I'm no longer going to skate with Sherri."

William felt a cold chill in his spine. He recalled Victor quitting hockey. Was he going to quit figure skating? "But why, son?"

Victor looked at Grandma. "Because I'm the star."

Relief flooded William's face.

That evening at the house, Ada explained everything to William and Mary, especially how their son had stood up for their honor.

Mr. Winters continually telephoned the house with his apologies. The practice ice time he'd already purchased had to be eaten by him. He did latch onto another young man to take Victor's place. Mr. Winters and his daughter were a closed book.

Victor's book, page by page, year by year recorded success upon success. Nothing in figure skating was insurmountable. Victor challenged every jump. Miss Rubin didn't understand what the driving force was within him. Did he have to master the movements to prove himself as an athlete or was there something more?

As Victor was making his name known across the country, he was also making his new sponsor, a Kennilworth widow, proud. Miss Rockwell enjoyed watching him skate, she was coming more and more to the rink. Outside of her cats, skating was her only passion. She remained anonymous to Victor - she neither wanted nor needed anything in return. Her only glory would be in the winning of Olympic medals for her country. She had the money to spend as she chose and it made sense to her to spend it this way rather than taking it to the grave. Only Miss Rubin knew her identity. Many times Ada had talked to her, never knowing of her role, thinking of her as a sweet little old lady who enjoyed watching figure skating.

CHAPTER SIX

Time marched on. Ada grew older. Victor matured. Mary and William's love grew deeper. Eddie was on the police force. Tommy was enrolled in law school. Mel kept the books for the Four Blind Mice enterprise and he couldn't believe how successful his accomplices were. The other three partners weren't aware that Mel gave himself only $1.00 per year. The newsstand and hot dog cart owners were known to everyone.

One summer night, business was slow. The only people out were drunks from the Lucky Lady bar across the street. Ian and Ed had time to argue about baseball. Ed was a die-heart Cubs fan. Ian was a Boston Red Sox enthusiast. Even though he'd never seen the game, it was his pride to say Boston had the better team. Ed, who had seen many Cubs games before the war, preached it was this year they'd win the pennant.

In the middle of the squabble two drunks ordered hot dogs. After getting them, they complained, "We aren't going to pay for this garbage."

Ian said, "Fine. Give me back the hot dogs."

The drunks harassed Ed and Ian. Suddenly they became quiet. They paid Ian his money. All Ed heard was, "Don't ever bother them again."

As Ed and Ian were trying to thank their benefactor, there was only silence. Ed got a chill down his spine.

The incident was forgotten until their weekly card game. The women were upstairs gossiping and they overheard Ed telling the scene with the drunks. The ladies were upset.

Willis explained she was going to get on John's case, where was a cop when they needed one?

Ada said nothing. Smiling to herself, she knew she could handle the problem.

And she did. On William's birthday, Ada announced she had made arrangements for William to get a seeing eye dog. The dog was being trained in Morristown, N.J. She was also giving

Mary and William a vacation to Morristown so he could work with the dog.

Ed explained to William that he'd have to be careful with the dog, "Those Chihuahuas are awfully small."

Mary had a wonderful three weeks with William. It was her first real vacation. Even though they were in a strange environment in an unknown place, it was like the honeymoon they'd never had.

It was work for William. He got to know his new friend, Misty April. As he learned to walk with the dog, Mary was always waiting for him.

Misty was a beautiful dog: alert, trim, muscular, and very obedient. When the training was completed, Ada flew to New Jersey to help the trio return home.

When they walked into their house, everybody was there to greet them. All their friends, and especially Victor, wanted to meet the newest addition. Misty took it in stride, the dog instinctively recognized the love of the guests, although she herself looked ferocious.

William may have been Misty's owner, but it was the woman of the house who fed and groomed the dog as the man enjoyed walking with her.

It was only a couple weeks before the dog knew her turf and the people who belonged on it.

At the paper stand, it was different. Because it was her domain, she got to know her two other godfathers and establish her dominance.

One day Ian put on the sidewalk next to the cart, a box of hot dogs. As he was putting them into the steamer, he realized he had been cheated: seven hot dogs were missing. He complained to William to tell Mel that he had to count the hot dogs when he bought them. This happened three and four times. Mel explained to Ian that he did count the hot dogs, they were all accounted for.

As happens so often in life, the innocence of youth reveals the truth. A little girl and her mother were walking by as the girl said, "Mommy, look at the dog eating hot dogs."

Ian heard this, put his hand down, and felt a gigantic head munching. "Ed, I think I caught the thief. I know why I'm missing hot dogs. It's got a big head, big ears, and an even bigger appetite. William, you got yourself a thief for a dog."

For the two-three hours that their shifts overlapped, William now had to watch the dog as well as the newsstand.

Another problem involved Misty. Ed discovered she loved hot peppers. She'd whine and whine for more.

One weekend Victor had a competition in Minnesota. Ada drove him. William and Mary looked forward to a relaxing, romantic interlude. They had just retired to the bedroom, not wanting to be disturbed by man nor beast. The whining started and continued, but was ignored by William. Finally it stopped. William eventually got out of bed to see what was wrong.

In the living room, he called out, "Mary did you buy bananas?"

"No, dear. Why?"

"Well, I just stepped on something. It feels like a cold, mushy banana."

Mary joined William. He knelt down on one knee. "No, Mary, it's not a banana. It's dog shit..."

Mary laughed at William's predicament. "If you weren't as horny as Rudolph Valentino, you would have walked your dog. She's your dog, you clean up the mess."

"I should get Ed here to clean the mess. He's the one feeding her peppers."

Sunday evening, Ada and Victor returned. Ada smiled from ear to ear. "Well, ladies and gentlemen, Victor has received an offer too good to refuse."

"What Mom?" Mary asked eagerly. "I hope it's not to skate in pairs again."

"Oh no. William, what's the greatest competition your son could compete in?"

"He's going to the '88 Olympics?"

Ada maintained her composure. "You got it. He was spotted in Minnesota and was invited to the try-outs. Miss Rubin knows he can qualify for the team."

William stood with tears in his eyes. He yelled out, "Victor."

Victor was upstairs rough-housing with Misty. As he came down, his father extended his arms for a hug. As both men patted each other on the back, they knew their dreams had come true. The women also stood with tears glistening in their eyes, knowing William had touched the top of the rainbow. All the unhappiness of the past was forgiven by the word "Olympics."

Of course, Ada went to her bedroom to call Sr. Richard so the parents could enjoy the moment of triumph with their son. Sr. Richard gave Ada her recognition, too. "You know, Ada, there are grandmas, and then there are Grandmas. If Victor makes this, I want you to enjoy his success. Without you, this would never have occurred. That boy has a special angel and that's his grandma."

Ada's eyes were moist from tears - but not tears of joy at Victor's chance, but from the tribute by Sr. Richard of having done her job well.

Miss Rockwell heard the news from Miss Rubin. She was as excited as if she held the winning ticket in the Kentucky Derby. Even though she wanted no credit, the feeling inside of her could not be dismissed. She told Miss Rubin that if more ice time was available to get it and double the training which Miss Rubin did. Ada didn't have the time to go to the restaurant to gab. It was constant training for Victor. Victor took to it like a duck to water. The harder the training the more he loved it.

In secrecy Miss Rockwell asked that in his performance Victor skate to the music, "Malaguena." It was a small price to ask for the thousands of dollars she had spent on his training. As Victor skated through his routine, Miss Rockwell empathized with the music and Victor. Ada sat with her, still unaware of her identity and gossiped about her family history. Every once in a while, Ada would say, "I'd like to know who the sponsor is."

Miss Rockwell replied, "It's probably a Chicago gangster who needs it as a tax break."

Ada simply smiled, "I hope God takes gangsters into consideration."

As Miss Rockwell listened to tales of Victor's background and family situation, she felt her money was being used for a noble purpose.

As time goes by, life has its ups and downs. The up was Victor continued to improve. The down came one morning when William went to wake up his mother and found her lying still and cold, peacefully at rest. She had passed away during the night from a heart attack. William was in shock. Everyone who knew her was in pain. She did so much for her family and asked for so little. As Mary sat back, she remembered thinking many years ago that this was the woman who would interfere in her marriage, but it was just the opposite. Ada strengthened her marriage and happiness.

Victor took it worse than anyone. Once again someone close had deserted him, vanished without a good-bye. He was more shocked and depressed than his father, especially when they were in Ogdensburg to bury her. The hearse carried Ada's body. Mel rented a van to drive Ada's friends and family, except John who couldn't leave. He was the security for their homes and with help from his friends, kept the stands going.

While at the cemetery, after the service Victor needed to be alone. He walked through the grounds and came upon a mausoleum engraved with the family name "Victor Wolf." Seeing it snapped him out of his reverie. He called Eddie and June over to him. They stood staring at the name. June had a chill run down her spine.

"Do you think that's any relation to the Coach?" Eddie mumbled.

June told them, "It's just a coincidence."

On the drive back to Chicago, June was haunted by Ada's amazing relationship to the Coach. What had made Miss Ogdensburg so special to him?

If ever there was a right or wrong time to die, this was the worst time for Ada to pass away. Victor needed her more than ever - not just for her driving, but her motivation and excitement had been contagious. Miss Rubin may have been his coach and had taught him well, but Grandma had been his source of encouragement.

In the tryouts, his compulsories were executed perfectly. But in his free style routine, Victor was pushing too hard to win. His heights on his jumps were outstanding, but he couldn't land them. He fell twice. In this competition, falling even once disqualified a contestant. When it was all over, Victor hadn't qualified.

On the plane trip home, Miss Rubin consoled him. He had tried too hard. She complimented him on his fifth place standing, "That tells me the next time you'll place higher."

"I don't know if I want to try for the next Olympics. I gave it all I could."

Miss Rubin stared into Victor's eyes. "What do you think your Grandma would say if you had said that to her? All that work and trophies mean nothing? Because you lost the battle doesn't mean you've lost the war. Isn't that what your Grandma would have said?"

"But I went out to win this for her."

"I know you did, Victor. I know you pressed too hard, you weren't relaxed. Let's give your Grandma four more years. I know you can win."

Then Victor stared off into space. His thoughts went back in time. Moe - would Moe have quit? He also remembered Moe's father on the ice, telling the hockey players, "Anybody can quit. Anybody can lose. But can you ask yourselves, did I do my best? Did I really want to win? If you can answer yes, it may not bring victory, but you can walk out of the locker room with your head held up high."

Victor looked at Miss Rubin, "Let's give it four more years."

When Victor returned home, it was painful telling his Dad he hadn't qualified.

William could tell by the sound of his voice he was upset. "You know, son, there were many times in crucial games, I shot the puck. My team could have won, but I missed the goal. My coaches always told me there would be another time."

"But, Dad, I wanted this so much for Grandma."

William smiled. "The one thing we can say about your Grandma is she always got up and tried again. And she wasn't an athlete. But she was like the Rock of Gibraltar."

"I can guarantee you, Dad, in four years, I'll be there."

Both men embraced each other. Victor looked at his mother. "The good news, Mom, is that you don't have another trophy to dust."

"It'll be there someday. The only trophy I worry about is you."

"You don't have to worry about me, Mom."

"Is that so? Well, I do worry about how you're going to do in college. I know how difficult it's been for you since Grandma's died. But your Dad and I have gotten you something we know will help a lot. We weren't able to get it for you on graduation day. Grandma left us a little inheritance and we used it to get you a car. When you go to Northeastern in January, you won't have to take the bus."

"But, Mom, I don't have my license."

"You did have driver's ed and you passed. Getting it should be no problem. Maybe Eddie can take you out practicing a bit and go with you for your test."

That's exactly what happened: getting his license would be an unforgettable event. Since it was early morning, Eddie asked his Dad if he'd like to go to the Elston Ave. licensing facility. Because the facility also issued state photo ID cards, Eddie thought it was a good idea for his father to get one. Eddie, who had to renew his driver's license, was dressed in his police uniform when he and his father picked up Victor.

Eddie only needed to take his eye test and get his photo taken. While he waited for his license, he helped Ed fill out the forms and get his photo taken.

Victor breezed through the written test and the driving test.

Two newly arrived Mexican men took their written driver's test in Spanish and were waiting to be called for their driving tests.

After he finished his dad's forms, Eddie went to the bathroom. While he was gone, the clerk who handed out both the ID cards and driver's licenses called the names on the finished documents. The Mexican men didn't know that ID cards were issued and so they stared in disbelief: if a blind man could get a driver's license, they knew they weren't going to have any problems.

Getting his license gave June a break from driving Victor to his training sessions. Victor now drove William and Ed to their weekly bowling games. He hung around and learned to keep score. He even bowled with his father on occasion. He drove his mom to the grocery store. Victor assumed much of Ada's responsibilities.

Victor enjoyed the Tuesday night bowling. Uncle Ed was always doing something: peeking through a peephole in the women's rest room and embarrassing the women or feeding Misty April beer. Not only Ed, but everybody gave her the last few drops and soon the dog was an alcoholic. Misty enjoyed her beer so much that the mere sight of the bowling alley made her drool. Between the peppers and the beer, as well as all the other goodies, Misty was no longer sleek and trim.

Misty wasn't acting like her old self so Victor took her in to see the vet. He explained her background as a seeing-eye dog who loved food. The doctor's eyebrows rose when Victor mentioned she loved beer. The doctor scolded him for endangering the dog's health and the people who depended on her. The dog was too valuable to be overindulged by acts of human kindness. The excessive snacking had to be stopped. Victor silently accepted the blame and shielded the real culprits.

When Victor brought home Misty and told Mary about the doctor's advice, Mary laid down new rules: no more beer, no more goodies, and a lot more walking.

All three men felt responsible for Misty's condition. They agreed with Mary not to spoil the dog. Yet each man felt sorry for poor, hungry Misty. Secretly each slipped her goodies. Ed, knowing how good a cold beer tastes, managed to drain the last few drops of the golden brew into her bowl. Even Victor cheated. It seemed the rules and regulations to reduce Misty's weight were violated by everyone, except Mary. Misty weighed more than ever. When Mary placed the dog food in her bowl, she noticed Misty wasn't eating as much as before. Mary thought the improved diet and walks were doing the trick.

When Mary and Victor took Misty in for her follow-up visit, Mary was so proud of the good job she'd done. The vet was shocked at Misty's weight. "You know, Mrs. LaBuld, if this keeps up, your dog is not going to live. Right now she has an ulcer which I suspect is aggravated by the hot peppers and beer. Is it fair to cause her needless pain?"

"Doctor, I have put her on a diet. It's the other people around her."

"Well, you'd better explain to these other people that if they want to have Misty around, they must stop feeding her."

On the way home, Mary told Victor to tell everyone that Misty was dying, but she could live a little longer if she stayed on a strict diet and lost some weight and exercised more.

The three guilty men decided to do something about Misty's condition. Ian let Ed handle the hot dog cart as well as the paper stand while he walked Misty around the block.

She felt as if she were in training for a track meet. She cried and whined for hot dogs and peppers. Misty scooted her water bowl to Ed, hoping for a shot of beer. When William took her for another walk, Misty laid down and refused to budge another inch. Ed had to pay a boy to carry Misty back to the hot dog stand. She was out of shape and was quite content to stay that way. Misty cocked her head and pleaded with her big brown eyes, but the men stood their ground. The worse torture was the bowling alley. She couldn't have even a nip of beer. Slowly the dog lost the excess weight.

For the next three years, Misty continued to fight the battle of the bulge. Victor was going to college as he continued training for the Olympics. William and Mary's love grew stronger. But Grandma Ada was still missed.

At the Lincoln Restaurant, a new waitress, Mary Jo, started working. At first she couldn't understand how these handicapped people could enjoy life so much. But after a while, she requested the Tuesday night shift so she could be their waitress. She began to understand their joy of living and she looked forward to Ed's antics and remarks.

One Tuesday, when Victor came to pick up William and Ed, Mary Jo noticed what a handsome young man he was. Eventually they got into a conversation. Victor mentioned he was a figure skater. Mary Jo told him that her daughter Suzette also figure skated.

At home, Mary Jo asked her daughter if she knew about Victor LaBuld. Suzette told her he was good enough to be the next gold medalist at the Olympics. Mary Jo's last wistful thought was, "If I was only twenty years younger!"

Now every Tuesday night, Mary Jo saw her daughter at the restaurant. Being a waitress is a lot like being a psychiatrist - you quickly reason why things happen. As Suzette watched the clock, much like Cinderella, at the appointed hour three blind men and their good-looking bodyguard appeared. Suzette nudged her mother to introduce her to Victor. As soon as they were introduced, they couldn't stop talking to each other, just as William and Mary had done those many years ago at Ashland and Irving Park.

Victor adopted a new routine on Tuesday nights. Instead of quietly studying while waiting for his Dad and Uncle Ed, he talked with Suzette. One night, Ed walked by their booth and heard them talking. Ed asked Mary Jo, "Who's that hooker Victor's talking to?"

"That hooker is my daughter."

Unashamedly, Ed warned her, "You'd better watch out for that young man. He's a regular magician: he can have her bra strap off in less than ten seconds. Promise me you'll make him keep his hands above the table, clapping at all times."

Mary Jo simply smiled. "Didn't I hear many a tale from you that no one ever had to worry about figure skaters, since most of them didn't fly right?"

Her logic dumbfounded Ed.

As Victor and Suzette talked shop, Victor asked, "Did you ever know a Victor Wolf?"

"Yeah, I hated him. He was so cocky on the ice. And his father! On Sundays I used to peek and watch the hockey players practice. He was kind of scary."

"Not really. He knew a lot about hockey. But Moe was my friend."

"Moe?"

"I mean Victor."

"What do you mean - was your friend."

"He disappeared after his father died. Well, that's a long time ago."

"You know, Victor, I was never jealous of you."

"Why's that?"

"You never looked down on your opponents. You always shook their hands. Your friend Moe took his trophy and laughed at the rest of the world."

"He wasn't laughing. He was daring everybody to beat him. He gave everybody a challenge, including myself. As his father would say, 'You have to want to be a winner.' "

"Well, I wanted to be a winner. I even wished I was the girl skating with you in the doubles instead of Sherri."

"That was a big mistake."

"Why?"

"That girl's father couldn't accept my parents' being blind. It was as though they had leprosy."

"My mother thinks your Dad and Ian and that funny guy Ed are the wackiest people she's ever met. She even told me if she could, she'd love to steal the dog."

"You mean Misty?" Victor smiled. "What would your mother want with an overweight dog who's a recovering alcoholic? She could never steal that dog because she'd always find her way home - she's the queen of the castle."

William and Mary felt a new glow of happiness surrounding Victor. He was on the phone to Suzette for hours on end. Besides figure skating and school, Victor enjoyed dating Suzette.

Mary's curiosity was in high gear. She was dying to meet Suzette. Finally Victor agreed to bring her home for a quiet little supper. But everybody's curiosity snowballed it into a full-blown party, with Ed and June and Willis and Ian.

From the moment Suzette entered the house, she was probed by the combined feminine forces. They slyly asked her opinion on the most important subjects, matrimony and motherhood. Although she never studied for the test, Suzette passed with flying colors. She was impressed with Mary's dinner. She couldn't believe a blind woman could prepare such a feast. Suzette didn't have much of a chance to eat. Ed had been warned to keep his humor clean and respectable.

Suzette's eyes were opened to the love of this diverse family, especially towards Misty. No wonder the dog was overweight. Everyone was slipping her food under the table. The sighted people would never tell, they were just as guilty. The unsighted never knew, they carried their own guilt.

Suzette had been nervous when Victor first invited her to dinner. But after an hour of being in the midst of blind people she realized they were just people - they were no different than sighted people. She was at ease with them and enjoyed herself. The family readily accepted Suzette. What she didn't know was Victor was being just like Ada, silently watching how she reacted to their blindness.

Suzette insisted on helping Mary with the dishes. As they washed and gossiped, Mary mentioned the annual picnic at the Lighthouse. She invited Suzette and Mary Jo to it. June would be running the sno-cone machine and Willis was going to help with the cotton candy. When Victor walked into the kitchen and heard them discussing the picnic, Mary wanted to know why Victor hadn't already invited her. He sheepishly grinned and gave both of his loves a peck on their cheeks before he returned to the living room.

As Victor drove Suzette home, she asked him, "Am I invited to that picnic?"

"Yes, but you got to understand it's mostly blind people."

"So?"

"It doesn't bother you to be around blind people?"

"Does it bother you that my mother's a waitress and that she worked two jobs just so I could figure skate, even though the possibility of being a champion wasn't there for me. Between the Social Security I got till I was eighteen and my mom's tips, we barely managed to make it. But she made sure I had my figure skating. A lot of those other parents looked down on us because we didn't drive a fancy car or live in a ritzy house. We didn't have money for private lessons. My extra practice came at the public skating sessions or helping out in the figure skating clinics."

The rest of the ride home was silent as Victor smiled to himself. Victor wanted to tell her that his life was a bit better than hers: the unknown sponsor helped tremendously with the financing, but both their lives had the most important element - love.

When they reached her house, they stayed in the car to talk. Soon the talking stopped and their budding romance was in full bloom. This was a new world for Victor, he didn't realize how happy his parents were that he finally had a girlfriend. They gently maneuvered him at every opportunity. He wasn't prepared for these newly discovered feelings. Once unleashed, they were impossible to control. Besides discovering a woman's figure and profile, Victor discovered the city of Chicago. They went everywhere together: the lakefront, the zoo and museums, theaters, the Loop.

As they were at the top of the Sears Tower, looking down Victor felt a strange sensation. "Look how small those people below look. The men who built this had to be crazy to go up this high."

Suzette replied, "They must have no fear. Most of them were Indians, with a few crazy Irishmen thrown in."

"How do you know that?"

"My mother is a waitress."

"So?"

"So, the iron workers found a bar first, then a restaurant. She worked down the street and came home with unbelievable stories. But she had a crush on this one - the men called him Jr."

"Did you ever see him?"

"No, sometimes I think my mother made him up. Nobody could do everything she says he did."

The last Friday in June was a beautiful day. A perfect day for a picnic at the Lighthouse. Willis drove everyone, except Victor who picked up Mary Jo and Suzette.

When they arrived, Mary Jo asked if they needed tickets to enter. Victor explained that the Lighthouse held the old-fashioned picnic every year for the blind clients and their families. But this would be the last one because the Lighthouse needed the land for a new building.

Victor, Suzette, and Mary Jo found the rest of the party. They walked around the grounds, amazed at the openness of the people. One of the sighted instructors, Mr. Bikula, was face painting the children. Another lady was running games. Willis and June were working at their machines making goodies.

Mary Jo needed cigarettes. She went into the lobby to use the machine. As she quietly sat puffing on one, a blind man sat on her lap. She had been too quiet and he hadn't realized anyone was there. After he apologized for his error, he asked her if she could see. When she said yes, he enlisted her help in using the cigarette machine. He knew the vendor had filled the machine that morning, but the man sometimes moved the brands. She helped him get the brand he wanted. Mary Jo learned two lessons: make a little noise to let a blind person know you're there and don't be afraid to ask for help. When she told Victor of her adventure, he told her a few stories about another rule: don't move things out of their places.

After lunch, a blind band played. The quartet had been together a long time. Suzette noticed that one of the men established the beat by patting a woman singer's rear-end. The group was amazing. They played and played until another act relieved them.

Misty was in doggie heaven! All the food and so many willing hands. Ed was trying his hardest to make deals to mate the spayed Misty with other seeing-eye dogs. Suzette realized, as her mother already had, these handicapped people possessed a joy of life that others only dreamed of.

Mary Jo was received warmly into Victor's family. They liked her sense of humor as well as her honesty. She tended to over-help the blind and Mary gently explained that they appreciated the help, but they were independent enough to function on their own. The two ladies became close friends. One day, Mary told her how grateful William and she were that Suzette had come into Victor's life. Her own life had been empty until she met William. She knew that one day they would be gone and now Victor had someone with whom to share his life. Suzette had drawn him out of his shell into a life of happiness.

But Victor's happiness meant problems for figure skating. Miss Rubin was alarmed at the new Victor. She spoke to him and reinforced the commitment needed to earn a gold medal: nothing would be allowed to interfere with his training.

Again, Victor's roller coaster life was in a series of ups and downs. Another down came when Miss Rubin told him that his sponsor died. She finally revealed Miss Rockwell's name. Victor and his entire family attended her wake and funeral. Victor was devastated to have so much taken from him. The Olympics were six months away. There was no way he could train for the competition, complete his final year of college, and make plans for a future with Suzette. William and Mary realized that her death meant the end of Victor's dreams.

At the funeral luncheon, Mary and William told Victor they had managed to save some of the inheritance from Ada and would use it for figure skating because Grandma would have wanted it that way. Miss Rubin told him that he didn't have to worry about paying her coaching fees. She knew he could win the gold and she wasn't going to let anything stop him. The ice time and expenses could be paid with Ada's money.

Victor thought long and hard about his future. A few days later he discussed it with Suzette. He had decided to go for the gold, until she told him she was pregnant. Emotions churned within Victor. He knew where his responsibility lay: he would quit figure skating and college, get a job and get married to support his wife and child.

Suzette argued with him, she had saved enough from her job at the bank so they could get married and survive the year without Victor giving up everything that meant so much to him and his family.

Victor told her, "No. As much as I've worked for a gold medal, you and this baby are more important. We will get married."

The roller coaster had plummeted to its lowest point. Victor and Suzette gathered together their parents to make their announcement. As Victor began his carefully rehearsed speech, he was interrupted by a phone call. An attorney for Miss Rockwell was on the line informing Victor that she had left his family, Miss Rubin, and Ed and June a legacy. Victor couldn't believe it. This was the solution to his predicament. He held off his announcement for a better time.

The beneficiaries met in the lawyer's office for the reading of the will. The lawyer read a letter from Miss Rubin addressed to those assembled.

My Dear Friends,

I want to introduce myself to you. My name is Dolores Rockwell. I've been known to you as Victor's sponsor. I wanted to remain anonymous because I respect the sport of figure skating too much to get caught up in a world of chicanery. I wanted only to watch a budding skater develop into an accomplished artist. Yet I feel I've come to know this circle of family and friends. I sat with you and felt the blessings of the Lord. Through good investments and luck, I have become a rich woman. But I know I can't take it with me when I depart this earth. I have no other descendants and so Ada, the LaBulds, the Brunettis, and Miss Rubin became my surrogate family.

Ada, my confidant and also my gossiping companion, I wanted to thank for a friendship which I cherished because of its sincerity. She wanted nothing in return, we were simply two little old grandmas enjoying ourselves with a bit of gabbing and philosophizing.

Ed and June Brunetti, I would like to thank for your love of life. Ed's humor helped me appreciate a side of life I had never experienced. June is a true friend, she sacrificed her time, talent, and energy to help those who needed it.

William and Mary LaBuld, I was shown many lessons in courage. You never let blindness stand in your way. Your love for each other, your family, and friends shone like a beacon in the night.

Miss Rubin, I appreciated your commitment to create a star, although you yourself are a star in my eyes. Your understanding of the pressures an athlete must withstand has allowed you to shield Victor and allow him to concentrate on what he loves best.

Victor, if I could have had a son, it would have been you. Your love for your parents and family is unique in this modern world. You have a grace and agility on the ice that has to be presented to the public. I want you to continue with figure skating.

I am leaving you the bulk of my estate so you and those who love you will never have to worry about figure skating ice times, fees, or any other expenses.

When you win the gold, remember your Grandma and all of us who love you so dearly. God bless all of you.

In Love and Light,
Dolores Rockwell

The grief in the office was compounded by each person thinking to himself, "Do I really deserve this?" Each person remembering pain. Yet it seemed that God had found an angel to relieve some of the suffering. Each person asking himself, "Did I really give this person joy?"

To Mr. Jonscher, these self-doubts didn't change the bequests. As her lawyer, he'd drawn an air-tight will. Miss Rockwell's final happiness and dreams would materialize, nothing on this earth would interfere.

As they left the office, Victor drew aside Miss Rubin and asked her, "Why me?"

Miss Rubin explained, "You're a winner."

101

After Victor dropped off his parents, he went to Suzette. He smiled, dropped down on one knee and proposed to her. "Quit your job and come with me while I compete."

"But what about the baby? Shouldn't we tell our parents?"

"Not yet. Let's give them a chance to get over the shock of Miss Rockwell. We'll get married and later announce it to them." Then Victor related the events at the lawyer's office. Suzette thought it was just like the old-time television show, "The Millionaire." She thought of herself as a modern Cinderella and they would live happily ever after.

They found time to get married at City Hall. Mary Jo, William, and Mary attended the ceremony. Both sides understood Victor didn't have the time for a big wedding now. But the parents knew that once the Olympics were over, they would have a huge reception. More than ever, because of Miss Rockwell, everyone felt the commitment of Victor to winning. Victor had to postpone going back to college. The pressure and training times were too intense to allow him to continue his education.

Mary Jo felt the pangs of separation. Suzette was living at the LaBuld's. But she was pleased that her daughter was in love and married and happy. She was amazed how the Olympics consumed everyone. She, as well William and Mary, still didn't know Suzette was pregnant.

Miss Rubin, Suzette, and Victor traveled the country and Europe to skating competitions. Suzette was exhausted from morning sickness and the itinerary. She tried to attend every practice session. Finally the morning sickness stopped and she could talk to Miss Rubin and explain she wasn't sick because of nerves. Her suspicions confirmed, Miss Rubin waited for Suzette to continue. "I'm pregnant."

Miss Rubin hugged her as she whispered, "Congratulations. I'm so glad you didn't have a case of nerves." She lapsed into a world of contented thoughts. "Perhaps I'll live long enough to train another LaBuld champion!"

"Oh Miss Rubin, you'll live forever. Would you do us the honor of being the baby's godmother?"

102

For the first time, the tough-as-nails Miss Rubin allowed a tear of joy to trickle down her cheek as she smiled and said, "Yes."

As they traveled, the crowd in the stands knew they were watching a winner. Even in Europe, facing tougher competition and judges, the spectators loved him. He was a winning machine, except no machine ever smiled as he did when the announcer listed his scores or presented him as the winner.

Victor and Suzette frequently called their parents and sent them video tapes of Victor. Suzette always ran the camera so no one was aware of her condition.

William, Ed, and Ian were constantly bragging about Victor. They'd meet at Ed's house and although they couldn't see the film in the VCR, they felt the excitement of the crowds and Victor's performance. His star shone brighter than ever.

One day, Ed and William decided since their children were grown and financially secure, they could do something for themselves.

Following their weekly bowling, the men made sure that June, Mary, and Willis were at the Lincoln Restaurant. William and Ed proposed to Ian a new venture: running a restaurant. Ian was ill at ease because he didn't have enough money to become a partner. William explained that they had received a kindness, it was important for them to give a kindness - it really wasn't their own money they'd be using, it was Miss Rockwell's. Who better to share it with than their best friend?

Mary Jo hovered near and spoke up, "What about me? I sure would love to work in a place where the inmates were in charge."

Ed addressed her, "We're counting on you. Every restaurant needs a hussy. Besides that, you're kin."

Ian expressed his doubts, "Why should I be a partner?"

For the first time, Ed got serious with Ian. "Are you ignorant? You're a part of William and me. We've gone through some rough times and we've always pulled together because you said things would get better. If society says it's wrong for a man to say he loves another man, then we're guilty. We do love you, Ian. That's what God has given us. The restaurant is going to be family owned and ran. And you are family."

June, Mary, and Willis sat silently in total shock.

"Now let's get down to business, " said William. "Ed and I have figured out everybody's jobs: Mary Jo, waitress; Ian and June, cooks; and we'll have to hire another waitress."

"Can I apply now, William, for the waitress job? Or do I have to answer an ad?" asked Willis.

"What about your soaps on TV?"

"I think I'm getting into a soap and I wouldn't miss it for the world."

William continued, "Ed wants me to be the manager. And Ed is in a position to be named. Is this agreeable with everyone?"

Everybody, except one, was smiling. Mary piped in, "No. Everybody's got a job. But what's mine?"

From laughter and good cheer to silence the mood changed.

William soothed her. "Honey, we didn't think of a position for you because of the hospital. I never wanted to take that away from you."

"But you never thought about my health."

"What do you mean?"

"Too much radiation can mess up your eyesight."

Everyone laughed. Mary had taken over Ed's role as comedian.

"Are you sure?"

"I'm just like Willis, I wouldn't miss this for the world."

"What position would you like?"

"I'd like to be in the kitchen with Ian and June."

Ed spoke up. "Mary, you're going to mess up everything. That position was for William's girlfriend."

"Well, his girlfriend's going to have to wait in line. I have to watch the bank account. Besides that, she'd have to be blind to fall in love with a man like this."

As usual, Mel's law office took care of the paper work.

At the weekly card game, everyone heard Mel tell Ed, "Everything's okay. We finally got the liquor license."

"What liquor license?" June asked.

Ed explained. "The liquor license for the restaurant."

"You never said anything about serving alcohol."

"Nobody ever asked. Besides I have to have a position. I'm the only one here with a personality."

"What do you know about bartending?"

"I think I've paid my dues."

"Drinking the booze is not the same as serving it, Ed."

June detected a frown overtaking Ed's smile. She thought to herself, "He gave his country his eyes. He gave the children and me happiness. How can I deny him this little pleasure?"

June answered, "All right, Ed. You get your bar. But we're going to change things."

"Like what?"

"Mary Jo is going to work behind the bar with you. Is that a deal?"

"Deal," Ed agreed.

The remodeling of the restaurant was finally completed after a couple of months. Once again, Mel refused to take money for his efforts. But William and Ed insisted. They were not charity cases.

William laid it on the line. "You know, Mel, all these years you got us hot dogs and everything we needed. You did more than any friend should do. We have to pay you."

Mel was straightforward with them. "Don't you understand what you have given me? All I have ever done in life is go to school, become a lawyer and listen to other people's cases. I never gave back from my heart. I was just a lawyer. But when you two men came into my life, you made me feel like a hero, just like you two are. I didn't laugh. I didn't play cards. I didn't belong to anything. The people I have to deal with are more worried about their money, their real estate, and their prestige. By knowing you two, I'm closer to my wife than ever before. You gave me a family. You can't buy that."

"You are family," Ed replied. "But we have the money that was left to us by a special woman. And we have our pride, too. If we were poor now, we would say 'Thank you.' But we're not poor and we're telling you to take the money or you'll hurt our feelings."

"So be it." And the matter was closed.

CHAPTER SEVEN

Mary Jo's loneliness caused by Victor and Suzette's separation from the family intensified during the Christmas holiday. This was Mary Jo's first time being apart from her daughter. But being with William and Mary relieved some of the pain. Misty also missed Victor. She whined on his bed many nights. Although everyone had gathered at William and Mary's home for Christmas eve, the mood wasn't very festive until the phone rang. Victor and Suzette wished everyone a Merry Christmas. Some of the frustration diminished. Everyone knew this was what had to be if Victor were to win a place on the Olympic team.

Suzette talked to Mary Jo and later to Mary and explained to each that they had mailed presents, but she had a super, one-of-a-kind surprise for them, and they'd have to wait until they came down to Florida for the try-outs.

Everyone - William and Mary, June and Ed, Connie and Mel, Willis and Ian, and Mary Jo - boarded the plane just after New Year's. From the time William and Ed got on the plane, June and Mary knew they had something up their sleeves. They looked like a couple of kids that had stolen the teacher's apple. All they needed was a drink or two to put them in the right mood. Ed rose from his seat, and taking his carry-on bag which Mel had helped pack, went to the rest room.

The flight attendant insisted on showing him the way. She inquired, "Would you like me to wait by the door for you?"

"No, that's alright. I'll be able to find my way back."

"I'll wait for you anyway."

Ed figured she would say that. He was in the rest room for about five minutes when suddenly there was a little commotion further up the plane. William had gotten up from his seat and had purposely fallen when he'd tried to find his way by himself. The waiting flight attendant rushed to help William.

Ed emerged from the men's room wearing a jacket and hat and looking just like an airline pilot. He walked into the first class section and announced, "Hello, ladies and gentlemen, I'm your pilot. I hope your trip will be an enjoyable one. We'll be landing in Orlando within..."

Before Ed could finish his sentence, he was grabbed by the flight attendant. All the people on the plane were in shock - they grasped the sight of a blind man dressed as a pilot, holding onto his cane, greeting them as their pilot. The flight attendant could no longer contain her laughter. She explained to the passengers that it was a practical joke. They started smiling and couldn't help but feel how stupid they'd been. One elderly woman remarked, "I'm all for equal opportunity, but not when it involves my safety."

As the flight attendant led Ed back to his seat, she said, "Now Mr. Brunetti, please let's not have any more games. Alright?"

"Yes, ma'am."

June was mortified, but everyone else in the group thought it was one of the funniest pranks they'd ever seen. When they disembarked, the pilot and co-pilot saw Ed and William in the terminal and congratulated them on their original caper. "It rates right up there with W.C. Fields!"

When the group arrived at the hotel, Mary Jo, Willis, and June helped everyone unpack. Willis was having a grand time, but she felt sorry for John who volunteered to stay home and dog sit. She didn't know John was showing off Misty to his buddies. Misty missed her owners, but was compensated with extra hand-outs from John's friends.

The big surprise was revealed that evening in the hotel dining room. Miss Rubin was already there. When Victor looking as dapper as ever and Suzette looking like an inflated blimp entered the room, they were greeted by Mary Jo's shriek of "Oh, my God!"

Mary instantly responded, "What's wrong?"

"Oh, my God. We're going to be grandmas!"

"Are you sure, Mary Jo?"

"It's either that or she's on Misty's diet."

Mary Jo hugged Suzette.

108

"What do you mean you're going to be a grandma? If you're a grandma, I'm going to be a grandpa. Oh my gosh! I'm going to be a grandfather," exclaimed William as he grabbed Ed and shook him. Victor then hugged his Dad, followed by everyone at the table. But Victor and Miss Rubin couldn't stay for the meal, they had to get to the ice arena for the competition.

When the group had settled down from their initial shock, the conversation centered on not only the new baby but also the past.

Suzette thought aloud, "We have so much to be grateful for. I wish I could have met Miss Rockwell. It it weren't for her, we wouldn't be here."

Mary continued her train of thought, "Actually we should remember Ada's role in all of this. Without her, where would we be?"

William went back one step further. "Let's not forget Moe. It was Moe who started Victor on this path. If he didn't interest Victor in figure skating, we'd have nothing but a beat up, bruised, toothless, crooked-nosed hockey player for a son."

Mary asked incredulously, "Is that you talking, William?"

"Yeah, is that you talking?" Ed said. "We'd better get away from this table before the ceiling crashes down." In his typical last-word-of-the-conversation style, Ed topped them all "If you really want to know who's responsible for all of this, it's me! I'm the one who let William sit alone on the bus. I'm quite a matchmaker."

June seriously added, "Actually, I would say it was Moe's father who made Victor a winner. Wasn't it Coach Wolf who inspired him when he needed it? But I still say, no disrespect to the dead, that man gave me the creeps!"

Willis saw everyone so involved in the conversation that she reminded them the clock was ticking away and they'd better hurry and eat or they'd miss the competition.

When the group arrived at the stadium, the other spectators stared at them and, as usual, wondered what blind people were doing there.

As the other skaters performed their routines, William and Ed, as they had done at countless performances, discussed the restaurant. Ian didn't want to listen to any more shop talk. He focused on the new sounds and the excitement of the competition while keeping his fingers crossed for Victor.

The loud speaker announced Victor's name. The men hushed. If there was a bookie around, he'd wouldn't have found a taker - Victor LaBuld was the odds-on favorite as well as the crowd's favorite. It seemed Victor had the competition sewn up, the performance was merely a formality.

Although Sr. Richard couldn't be there, her thoughts and prayers were with Victor as she turned on the TV to watch the try-outs with Sr. Bertha and the rest of the nuns.

Strains of music flooded the quieted arena. The spotlight focused on Victor's entrance. His jumps, especially the difficult triples, were flawless. His spirals made him appear as strong as an eagle but as graceful as a swan. He was no longer a diamond in the rough. Every movement out-shone the previous: his apparent ease disguised his strength and agility. His smile was not cocky, his face gleamed with enjoyment and a true love for the sport. He was surrounded by confidence.

His routine perfectly interpreted the music. Both music and execution were perfect. As he came to the closing sequence, he lunged into the air for a triple and missed. The oohs and ahs from the crowd upset the blind and Mary frantically asked June, "What happened?"

June tried to calm them, "Victor fell on his final triple. But he's getting up and finishing. He doesn't look hurt, just shaken up."

As Victor took his bow, the crowd responded with a standing ovation.

Anguish covered his face as he skated to Miss Rubin. "Do you think I blew it?"

"No, Victor, I think your level of difficulty will compensate for the fall. I think you made the team."

Miss Rubin was right. After all the performances were finished, Victor had won his spot.

In his dressing room, Miss Rubin noticed Victor rubbing his arm and chest. He dismissed it as a bruise, but she insisted he go to the emergency room to have it x-rayed. His family and friends consoled him. Miss Rubin drove Victor and Suzette to the hospital while the rest of the group returned to the hotel.

After the x-rays were taken, the doctor entered the examining room with an anguished look on his face. He asked Victor if he had a personal physician back home. When Victor told him no, the doctor gave him the name of Dr. J. Theodore King in Oak Park and told Victor to call him as soon as he returned home. He would inform Dr. King to expect the call.

"But why, Doctor Kane? Is there a problem?"

"There may be. These x-rays indicate something more serious than bruises. There's a shadow on your lungs. I don't want to alarm you, but it needs to be looked into by a specialist."

Numbly, Victor took the paper. He asked, "Doctor, are you sure? I've been healthy all my life."

"No, I'm not sure. That's why I want you to see Dr. King."

"Doctor, I would prefer you keep this quiet from my wife. Can we keep this between us?"

"No problem, Mr. LaBuld."

As Victor left the examining room, his face masked the news he had heard. He reassured Suzette that the bruises would soon heal, he just needed a little rest.

When they returned to the hotel and their waiting family, Victor told them the same story. They dismissed the distraught look on his face as disappointment. They reassured him that since he had made the team, he would bring home the gold. All the while his thoughts remained riveted to the doctor's words.

The family returned home ahead of Victor.

On the homebound flight, Miss Rubin kept encouraging Victor to look forward to winning and to put the fall behind him. Yet these words fell on deaf ears. Victor's inner turmoil never surfaced.

Victor and Suzette felt relief at being able to stay home. Both were exhausted.

After a few days rest, Victor and Suzette went to the new restaurant. When they walked in, all the customers already knew who they were. All Victor heard was, "He'll do it in France!"

William was proud of his son. Once in a while, he'd slip and mention that Victor had also played hockey.

A few days passed. Victor called Dr. King to set up his appointment. He was told to come in immediately. He left without saying a word to anyone.

The receptionist knew the name of Victor LaBuld. She asked him to sign four autographs. Then she gave him the medical history form to fill out. As soon as it was completed, the nurse led him into an examining room.

As he waited, the door opened and a young man in a blue lab coat complete with stethoscope entered and introduced himself. "I'm Dr. King, Victor. I didn't get a chance to see you on TV, I was at the hospital. But I got a call from Dr. Kane in Florida. He told me the situation."

"He could be wrong. Couldn't he, doctor?"

"Yes. That's why we're going to run some tests in the hospital."

Then Victor disrobed and the poking and prodding began. It seemed Dr. King knew exactly where to go and what to look for. When he pressed on Victor's chest, he flinched.

"Did that hurt?"

"It's where I fell, doctor."

"Oh, okay." But Dr. King kept returning to that spot.

Dr. King arranged for Victor to check in the hospital the next day.

Victor again had the doctor promise not to tell anyone.

As Dr. King left the room, Victor got dressed. As he was about to leave, he noticed a framed poem on the wall.

The Shepherd
By Victor Wolf

The air is warm
The sky is clear
You walk beside me
I have nothing to fear.

112

You are wiser than any man I know.
The love you give me always shows.
There are times you whine and cry.
But always you are mine.

I took your womanhood away
Now you have no puppies with which to play.
To honor me you've given me your very soul.
I'll never let you go.

Without you I can't see
Specially when the light turns green.
I honor you with a biscuit or bone
For your glory that no one knows.

At one time in life I could see
But war, hatred, money and self-esteem
Changed everything for me.
I cursed the Lord because I lost my eyes.
I shamed myself by being alive.
Then you came into my life.

You had no anger
You had no fight
You gave me your eyes
And showed me the light.

You are not like man destroying the world.
You lay by my side as a friend who guides.

If dogs have a heaven
There's one thing I know
God will wink His eye
And you will certainly go.

The poem was authored by Victor Wolf...could there be another Victor Wolf? Victor had to ask, "Dr. King, before I go, can I ask you something else? That poem on the wall says it's written by Victor Wolf. Is he a hockey player?"

"Yes, he is. Do you know him?"

"If it's the same Victor Wolf, I do. Is he just about my age?"

"Oh no. He's a much older man. He was a hockey coach."

"Was he a soldier also?"

Dr. King looked long and hard at Victor. "Yes, he was."

"Could you give me his phone number or tell me where he lives?"

Dr. King put his arm on Victor's shoulders. "I can't do that, Victor. It's against the rules. But your next appointment will have to be late in the evening, because Victor Wolf always has the last appointment of the night."

Driving home, Victor told himself that it couldn't be, the Coach was dead. Once he got home, he had a difficult time telling everybody he had to go into the hospital for tests. He also had to tell Miss Rubin he had to miss a few days practice. He explained that he might have a fractured shoulder from the fall.

Suzette had the advantage. She read the emotion he was trying to hide. No fracture could cause this. She feared it was something more.

Victor and Suzette arrived early at West Suburban Hospital. Everyone from the admitting office to the nurses and technicians were pleasant and accommodating. Suzette thought it was because he was a celebrity, but she soon observed that all the patients were treated with respect and dignity. The only drawback was they wanted his autograph.

She spent the whole day with Victor, leaving him only during tests.

Back at the restaurant, motherhood was nagging Mary. She worried about how Victor's fracture would heal. They wanted him to be healthy. The Olympics ran a poor second to his health. Everyone shared her concerns.

For the first time, Ed didn't wise crack. He loved Victor and couldn't say or do anything to detract from the seriousness of the situation.

Mary Jo had a wide open field. She told everyone, "I've had dozens of fractures in my time. They don't take no time at all to heal."

William fell into her baiting. "How'd you get so many fractures?"

"I was a lady wrestler."

Everyone politely smiled. But Ed perked up. "Did you win or lose?"

"I was always the winner. I had weaklings like you to deal with."

"You only won because you didn't use deodorant."

Everyone continued to smile, but Mary Jo realized their hearts were at the hospital.

Mary and William couldn't stand being away from Victor any longer. They went to the hospital while the rest of their cronies stayed to run the restaurant.

Every time a technician, nurse, or doctor examined Victor, his family inquired what the test was for, but never was given a definitive answer, "We're still looking into it" or "Dr. King needs all the information before he can make a diagnosis."

His family and friends took turns staying with Victor.

Early on the third day, a troubled Dr. King entered Victor's room and pulled a chair next to the bed. "Good morning, Victor. How did you sleep last night?"

"I've been too worried to sleep, Doctor."

"Victor, I'm going to be straight up with you. You have lung cancer. It's much more serious than we thought."

"What sort of treatment is there?"

"Unfortunately, it's too advanced. The most we can do is give you medication for the pain."

"How much longer do I have to live?"

"It could be six months to a year and a half."

Victor threw his head up in the air and stared at the ceiling. "Why has God done this to me, doctor? What have I done so wrong? I'm an athlete. I've taken care of myself."

"I don't have an answer for you, Victor. But I'm in your corner. Understand that."

"What about my parents? What about my wife? She's going to have our baby. Now I'm not going to be around to see the baby grow up. Why am I being punished?"

Dr. King sat, head down, in deep thought. He had no answer for this young man. But he knew he had to be strong for Victor to lean on.

Victor looked at Dr. King and asked, "When can I go home?"

"Tomorrow if you like."

"Remember, Doctor, I don't want my wife or family to know. They think I have a fractured shoulder. I'm counting on your discretion."

"Well, Victor, I'll see you tomorrow before you leave. We'll set up your appointment at my office. I'm sorry."

Victor laid with watery eyes as Dr. King left. Instead of going to his next patient, Dr. King went to the pay phone so he could privately call Victor Wolf. As the phone was answered, a rough, hoarse voice spoke, "Hello."

"Coach, it's Dr. King. How are you feeling?"

"I'm making it."

"I have a problem, Coach. There's a young man dying. He thinks he knows you."

"What's his name?"

"Victor LaBuld. You know, the figure skater."

"You didn't tell him I was alive, did you?"

"No, our secret's intact."

"What do you mean, he's dying?"

"He has cancer and it's moving fast on him."

"What can I do? That's God's worry."

"Victor, don't pull your toughness with me. Just imagine if your coaches would have said the same thing."

"They would have done me a favor."

"Were you a coach?"

"Okay, Doctor. What do you want me to do?"

Dr. King explained the situation.

"You know I do not like to be around people."

"Well, what if I come and pick you up and bring you to the hospital after visiting hours?"

"Okay, Dr. King, but why am I so special? I don't understand."

"I don't know either, Coach. But in my office, when he heard your name, his eyes glistened."

Very late that evening after visiting hours, Victor laid silently in his bed. He turned his head and saw a huge shadow filling the doorway. As it moved towards him, Victor's face changed from depression to delight. For the first time in days, his eyes sparkled. "Coach! Is it really you?"

"Yeah, Dr. King gave me a lift to the hospital. What, have I changed in all these years? Well, maybe I have - but I'm only thirty pounds overweight."

"You haven't changed, Coach."

"You'd better thank Dr. King for that. He makes me take this horrible medicine and I can't drink with it. But sometimes I fool him, I don't take it for a couple of days. Then I go off the wagon."

"But I thought you were dead."

"That's the way I wanted it, Victor. For six years I had to go to therapy and occupational therapy. I lost my balance, couldn't remember things, I was nothing but a cripple. God really put a zap on me."

"He put a zap on me, too, Coach. I thought I had the gold medal right in my hand. But He's taken it away."

The Coach pulled a chair right next to Victor's bed. "That bothers you, doesn't it? You think God has a vendetta against you. How do you think your father and your Uncle Ed felt when they lost their eyes? They probably said the same thing. And so have I. You see, a long time ago, I had the world in my hand. Hockey, baseball. I also had a close friend who was black. The reason we got along so well was that I was a foster child and he was the only black kid in the school. I felt I was nobody and he felt he was nobody. But if you put two nobodies together, they make a hell of a backfield in football. We told those people to kiss our ass. We laughed and had fun playing football. We had a dream we'd both be pros. We would have our families and live next door to each other and smile through life. But he had a car accident and died. I told everybody to stick sports up their ass. I

117

went to war, not caring if I lived or died. The war made me mean and nasty. But do you know what, Victor? I never denounced God because I know there is a God. Even when I fell from the beam. God was testing me. Now He took away all my talents from being a pile driver and iron worker. So I should hate Him, shouldn't I? I should denounce Him, there isn't a God. But then what happens? He sends me an angel - a Dr. King. One man that can understand me. You see, when I was young, I never liked the crowds."

"Why, Coach?"

"My friend and I would score. The crowds would pat us on the back. We were heroes. But just think, Victor, if we didn't play sports. Would they have known us? He was still a black kid and I was still a foster kid. Even though my foster parents loved me, I never felt it was my home. After the war I came back to Chicago. In between I played pro baseball and hockey. But I played without the love of the game. But as an iron worker, I worked on the Sears Tower. Have you ever been on it?"

"Yeah, Coach, my wife and I were."

"When you looked down, what did you see?"

"We hardly saw anything but little dots."

"Right. You see, as I hung on only a beam do you know what I realized? Everybody said the Sears Tower was going to be the tallest in the world. It deserved a first place cup. But it took all those little people to make it. They deserve all those first place cups. Look up in the sky. It's not really paramount. When you can shake hands with God, you'll know you've gone as high as you can go. As I hung from that beam, I knew God could breathe and blow me off any time He wanted. Do I make any sense to you, Victor?"

"Not really, Coach."

"Well, you think about what I've said. Fame and money isn't it. My own son has proven that."

"Moe, how is Moe?"

"Working and playing hockey."

"I always read the papers to see if he became a pro. I would have bet anything he would have."

118

"Yes, he could have been a pro. But instead of a contract, he stayed with a crippled man to help him get better. I'm sorry about that. But once again, that's how God had it planned. God made what people call the world. But actually it is a stage. And God wrote the script. Just like the Sears Tower and all those little dots. God knows each one and has a file on all of them. But remember one thing, there is no such thing as a bad God. He is your Creator. And He had your script ever since the day you were born.

"Victor, it's getting late. When you're out of the hospital, you come and see me." The Coach wrote his address and phone number, but told Victor not to tell anyone he existed.

Dr. King entered the room. He saw how Victor's face had come alive. "Are you comfortable? Is everything okay?"

"It's a little better."

Then Dr. King drove the Coach back to his apartment. On the way, Dr. King said, "I can't understand why all these young men admire you."

"It's simple, Doctor. I was a young man, too, once. Maybe I know where they're coming from. And maybe if they're headed in the wrong direction, I know it before anyone. I was one of those kids. This Victor LaBuld is one of the nicest kids on earth. But Fate has its course. I wish I could trade places with him."

"I don't want to hear that out of you, Coach. You've been spared because you still owe. Even though you're not teaching those kids hockey, there's going to be more Victor LaBulds that have problems. And they're going to need you. Remember, these are your own words: you have to balance off the scales. For all the evilness you did in Vietnam, you still owe the Man.

The Coach went back up to his apartment without saying a word. The world didn't know that the Coach didn't want to live. But Dr. King gave the Coach a purpose for staying alive, even if there was some trickery involved.

The next day when Victor left the hospital, there was more joyfulness in his face. The overwhelming task on his mind was how to tell Miss Rubin he was quitting figure skating. Replaying

119

in his mind the Coach's conversation, gave Victor the strength and courage to tell her.

Later that morning he drove to her home. She was delighted to see him.

Sitting in her living room, Victor began, "Miss Rubin, I'm no longer going to figure skate. I want you to call the Olympic Committee and let them send someone else."

"Why, Victor? Because you fell? You're quitting because you fell? Because you didn't come in first place? Since you were a little boy I saw a winner. Your Grandma believed you were a winner. Miss Rockwell recognized it also. You're going to disappoint all those people? Have you lost your courage?"

"Are you my friend, Miss Rubin?"

"I've always been you friend, Victor."

"You kept a secret for Miss Rockwell. Would you keep a secret for me, too?"

"Yes."

"I'm dying. I have been diagnosed with lung cancer. I have six months to a year and a half, maybe. Do you think I could concentrate on figure skating?"

Miss Rubin rose from her chair and put her arms around Victor. "Oh my God. I'm sorry, Victor. Are you sure?"

"I guess x-rays don't lie. I don't want my family to know, though I'm going to tell my wife."

Miss Rubin was in tears. "Victor, you have to let your parents know!"

"No, Miss Rubin. Last night in the hospital, an old friend came to see me. We talked and he made me realize something - what the value of love means. And knowing who you are, but never judge a book by its cover. If things weren't the way they are, I probably could win that medal. But does that medal mean I'm the best? My mother and father are the best. And my Creator. Miss Rubin, you will keep the secret, won't you?"

"Yes, Victor. But I want you to know you're the greatest pupil I ever taught."

They hugged each other.

When Victor left, Miss Rubin laid on her bed and cried. She wasn't crying for herself or that she hadn't succeeded in producing a winner. Her heart was broken because of the cruelty that life could inflict.

Victor couldn't wait a couple of days to talk to the Coach. He phoned him that afternoon and explained that he wanted to see Moe. The Coach told him Moe had a hockey game in Skokie after work.

That night Victor took Suzette to the Skokie rink. The Edens Expressway was clogged with rush hour traffic and they arrived late. As they entered, instead of a hockey game, there was a boxing match in progress on the ice.

After the referees broke it up, the loud speaker announced, "Five minute penalty for Joe Perillo and Victor Wolf for fighting."

All Victor could do was smile and remember. Nothing had changed.

Suzette was shocked at hearing the name Victor Wolf, but now she knew why they were watching a hockey game. "How'd you know Moe was playing here?"

"From an old, silent, wise man."

a week of moodiness, Suzette saw his face transform
down-in-the-dumps loner to a glow as bright as a
verse.

Moe stepped back onto the ice.
for him. Other teams preferred he sat in
stick. Yet as brutal as the game can
agility.
ited in the lobby while Victor
was amazed, time had stood
me as the Squirt team
scars, broken noses,

ed him on the
either.

you. I thought I'd
is is even better."

Then Joe Wood piped in, "I hear you're going to the Olympics. Nice going."

Victor looked at all his old friends. "We'll see. I'm not sure I want to go."

"You're not sure you want to go? Are you crazy? They say you're the best figure skater in the world."

Knowing the situation, Moe got them off the subject. "He's the only guy I ever had to bust my ass to beat. I'm glad he went to figure skating. If he didn't I wouldn't have been the high scorer all these years."

Victor smiled. "I could never beat you, Moe."

As the players dressed and bullshitted with Victor, they decided to go out after the game.

"Victor," Joe asked, "would you like to join us? We're going down to Rush Street to celebrate."

"Yeah," Moe continued, "come join your old buddies for a few beers."

"I have my wife with me. She's waiting outside."

"Well bring her along."

Victor thought, "Why not? There may never be a time like this again."

Victor was wrong about that. But this night was spe
Suzette was the only woman in the group and was pampere
the ruffians. Her opinion of hockey players did a hundred
degree turn, no longer thought of as nasty, drunk boors bu
as polite, considerate gentlemen.

Suzette watched Victor interact with his friends.
time and travels she'd known him, he'd never been
and truly exuberant. It amazed her that her hus
quickly assimilated into the group.

The first bar they frequented carded only Suz
They had never been in a real bar for seriou
closest was the bar at the Lincoln Restaurant.
wide-eyed innocence and asked what they'
they'd have whatever Moe was having. M
beer. Suzette had never drunk, even a be
getting tipsy. She used her pregnancy as

122

Coke. All the hockey team continued to drink beer until Joe yelled out, "The Coach is here. Sixty second drill!"

Then for the next minute each player started drinking shots as fast as he could, using beer as a chaser. The bartenders all knew this group: they were good for business because they guzzled those shots in sixty seconds and asked for more. But they also thought the animals were nuts. Victor and Suzette also thought they were insane.

Joe told them, "Every time we think of the Coach, we have to do something to get in shape! Did you ever see finer specimens than us? Don't you remember how hard he was, Victor?"

"Yeah, he was tough, wasn't he?"

"But he made hockey players out of us. From little kids, we stayed together. He always said one man's not a team."

"I remember that," Victor answered.

Moe turned his head to listen. But really only he knew his Dad.

In the next bar, Victor joined in when the sixty second drill was announced. At the third bar, the routine was repeated. But a reporter from a local newspaper called his office and a photographer came to catch on film an intoxicated, shot glass holding Victor LaBuld.

Thank God Suzette could still drive and help Victor into the house.

Mary and William were worried all night. When they saw Victor drunk, William's face smiled while Mary intensely scowled.

Before Mary could speak, Suzette explained, "Victor met his friend Moe and we went out drinking with him and the hockey team."

Victor, leaning on Suzette's shoulder muttered, "You should see them, Dad. The whole group has grown up and stayed together. Moe is still great. He skates like a rocket and his stick handling is better than most pros. I don't know why I ever left hockey."

Mary butted in, "Because you're the best figure skater in the world. And figure skaters don't destroy their bodies with alcohol. What would you Grandmother say? What will Miss Rubin say?"

"To hell with figure skating. To hell with Miss Rubin. I'm going to play hockey!"

"Suzette, put Victor to bed, please. He's losing it." As Suzette did so, Mary spoke up, "William, did you hear what Victor said - he's going to play hockey! You can blame yourself and Ed for being so rowdy at the bowling alley and drinking all those six packs at the house. No one in his sober mind would want to play hockey and be scarred and mangled for the rest of his life."

"Now, don't you knock hockey players. I was one. And I'm still beautiful. Just look at me!"

Mary's grin arrived. "If I could see, I'd probably put a bag over your head."

"Just make sure you give me two eye holes."

Mary went to bed peeved. William went to bed smiling, remembering how it was in his days with his friends.

The next morning, Victor was sicker than a dog. Suzette still smiled knowing Victor had a night of relaxation and time to relieve some of the pressures of the Olympic try-outs.

At the breakfast table, Mary jabbered away, "Victor, you're going to end up just like your Father and Uncle Ed. Nothing but a bunch of drunks!"

William waited for an opening. "Well, son, let's hear about the hockey game and Moe."

"He's great, Dad. He's better than the pros."

"Why didn't he go pro?"

"I don't know."

"Maybe it's because of his father's death."

Victor didn't answer. Mary listened and spoke out, "It sounds like he's turning out like his father - a little drunk." She put her head down. "I really didn't mean that."

The doorbell interrupted their conversation. Victor answered it and was greeted by three newsmen with microphones and cameras.

124

The first newsman asked, "Were you down on Rush St. last night? How can you be out drinking when you're supposed to be training?"

Victor slammed the door.

William yelled out, "Who is it, Victor?"

When he didn't answer, William himself went to the door. As he opened it, the departing newsmen turned and rushed the door again.

One reporter yelled out, "That's his father."

Another said, "Mr. LaBuld, why is your son out drinking and carousing when he should be training? Doesn't the gold medal mean more than just partying?"

William curtly responded, "I have nothing to say," and slammed the door.

Victor stood alongside his father. "I'm sorry, Dad."

"Sorry about what, son? A man's not allowed to have a drink without some sleazy reporters on his ass?"

Suzette and Mary joined them as William angrily continued, "Is this what the gold medal means? You don't have a private life?"

Mary explained, "William, that's what a star is. The public looks at him in a different light."

William added, "I love you, son, but if it's being a star and being millions of miles away from your friends and family, is it worth it?"

"Well, weren't you a star in hockey? Weren't you fighting to go to the pros?" Mary asked.

"That's right. But in hockey, you don't have one star. It's a team effort. When one man gets down, another picks him up. Who's here to pick up my son?"

Victor looked at him and smiled. "You are, Dad. If you thought I was drunk last night, I was. But I knew what I was saying. I'm not a quitter, Dad. But I want to see the world. I want to have some fun. All my wife knows is ice rinks. All you and Mom know is ice rinks. All I know is performing on an ice rink. Is that what life is? An ice rink? I saw Moe and his friends last night. They enjoyed living. Maybe that's why Moe

125

isn't a pro. Maybe he knows more than me. He's having fun. When he takes his skates off, he lives."

"But, Victor," Mary asked, "why do you think Miss Rockwell left us all that money? She wanted you to become a star and win a gold medal. What about Miss Rubin who's put all her time into you?"

"I guess I'm just a disappointment to everyone." Victor grabbed his mother's hand. "Mom, Suzette and I are going to have to leave here. There are going to be newspaper men here every morning and night. I meant what I said last night. I quit. As long as I'm in this house, there'll be an embarrassment, a scandal. But if no one knows where I am, they can't hurt or harass you or Dad."

"But how can you quit just like that, Victor?"

"Mom, I'm really tired. I'm not happy with myself. Are you and Dad happy with yourselves?"

Victor's words sunk deep into her heart. His happiness did mean more than a cold ice rink. As they hugged, Victor whispered, "I hope you'll understand someday."

Victor and Suzette ducked reporters as they quietly moved into their own apartment. All week Suzette silently observed her husband. There was something more on his mind. Finally she broached the subject. "Victor, what did you mean when you told your Mom you hoped she'd understand someday? I know you well enough to figure out there's something more. What's wrong?"

Despondent, Victor gazed into her eyes. "I think you made a mistake when you married me. I'm not going to be able to fulfill our dreams. I'm not going to be the star you thought I'd be."

"Oh, now you're trying to push me away. You can take that star and gold medal and pitch them out the window. I didn't fall in love with you for your trophies. I love you because of who you are, not what glory or prizes you get."

Victor looked straight into her eyes. "Suzette, I'm dying. I have cancer."

Suzette remained silent as the tears welled in her eyes. Finally she spoke, "How can you be sure? You're too young and healthy. There has to be a mistake."

Victor told her about the emergency room diagnosis and the hospital tests and the confirmation from Dr. King. "It's real, Suzette. That's why I had to quit figure skating. I want to live my life while I can. I want to see our baby born, but I know I'll never see him skate. I want us to be a family, but all that's been taken from me. I don't want my parents or anybody to know. I don't want them hurt. Promise me you won't tell anyone."

Suzette promised.

That night as Victor was sleeping, Suzette asked the Lord, "Why?" She kept thinking, "How much he loves us, trying to keep the hurt away from everyone. If he is so strong, I have to be just as strong. For however long we have together on this earth, I'm going to make sure he has the best time of his life."

For William and Mary, the time was filled with anguish. Finally they received a phone call from Victor who seemed to be hiding out like a wanted gangster, fearing reporters and unpleasant publicity. Each time his infrequent calls reopened their heartache. Suzette called Mary Jo, but kept the secret. Mary Jo slipped once in a while, "Doesn't Victor know how much he's hurting his parents and the people who love him?"

Suzette replied, "He loves his parents, but we have to live our own life. This is his choice and I am his wife. I have to stand by him. But don't worry, Mom. Things will work out."

Mary Jo wasn't the only one concerned. Down at the restaurant, everyone's heart went out to William and Mary. "They gave that kid everything and this is the way he repays them." "He's nothing but a quitter, even the newspapers said so." And on and on it went. It seemed that everyone abandoned Victor because he had deserted figure skating, his family, and friends.

Society says birds of a feather flock together. If Victor was a quitter, then he was going to see another quitter. With Suzette, they visited the Coach.

At first Suzette was apprehensive. She had heard some unsavory stories about the man. The apartment was nothing but trophies and plaques. As Victor and the Coach talked, Suzette read some of the material written by the Coach. As she read the poem, "The Shepherd," Victor caught her crying. He asked her what was wrong. She told him, "This poem sounds like Misty."

The Coach answered, "It is Misty."

"Is this the same poem in the doctor's office?" Victor asked.

"Yes, it is. Where your Father, Ed, and Ian had their stands, I used to sit across the street in the bar, drinking and watching the dog protect those three men."

"Why didn't you go over and say hello to them?"

"I'm a part of horror in a soldier's life. Your Father and Ed were soldiers. I can't let go of my memory. I can't let go of what I was. But I don't have to take anyone with me."

"I don't understand, Coach."

"One time in my life, I was no longer a human being. I was a machine. Matter of fact, even a butcher. Killing men meant nothing to me. I was always hoping it would be my last mission, that someone would shoot me and I could die with honor. But just like I tell you boys to obey your Coach, I obeyed my country, no matter what it took to win. But during this process, I never renounced my God. It's as though He has a little book with all my sins listed. For you see, Victor, life is like a scale. If you believe in a Creator, you know you have to balance those scales. I tried by teaching you boys hockey. But still it wasn't enough. I fell from a beam. I was actually a cripple. The Almighty took everything away - my coordination, everything."

Then the Coach grabbed him by the shoulder and squeezed. "But do you know what he didn't take? My faith. All those trophies, all those certificates, you can burn them. They'll disappear. But the one thing no one can burn is my soul. No matter what torture my Lord gives me, I will believe in Him. We all have to have something to believe in. He'll never design a building I can't scale to get to the clouds."

Then Victor smiled. "You mean like the Sears Tower?"

"That was nothing."

Suzette was pretending to read, but was really listening. His words took away some of her anxiety and gave her strength and understanding.

Then there was a slamming of the door and they knew who was home. Moe called out, "I'm home, Dad," as he walked into the living room. He had to eat quickly to get to a hockey game.

As he hugged Victor and Suzette, Moe asked, "Would you guys like to see another game?"

Victor didn't answer. Suzette smiled, "You bet. I'd even like to get in on that sixty second drill."

Victor put his fingers to his lips. The Coach didn't know the games the boys played.

When they got to the rink, Suzette waited in the bleachers while Victor went into the locker room to say hello.

There was a problem. There weren't enough men to play. Two were there, but had severe diarrhea - they'd been out all night drinking. Moe was pissed, that meant he had to tell the referees they were forfeiting the game, which he did. He went into the other team's locker room to inform them. The other captain asked Moe if they could play just for fun. To Moe, any game was good enough. But he had to okay it with the guys who had shown up. So he returned to his own locker room. "Hey you guys, they want to play a scrimmage game. They'll even lend us a couple of their men. Do you want to play or not?"

Joe was already dressed, so he said, "Why not?" Then he looked at Victor. "Hey, why don't you suit up?"

"I don't have any equipment."

"That asshole sitting there - the one with the shits - use his equipment."

"I don't think his skates would fit."

"Well, try 'em. What, have you forgotten how to play hockey?"

Moe looked at them. "He's been out of hockey a long time."

Victor's eyes lit up. "Let me see if his skates fit." The skates were a little big, but they were good enough. Victor smiled at Moe. "Let me give it a shot. I ain't got nothing to lose."

Moe shook his head and grinned.

Poor Suzette was still waiting in the bleachers for her husband. All of a sudden they came out on the ice. She thought she was hallucinating. There was Victor in hockey equipment, warming up with the other guys. Victor's timing with the stick was off. But he was trying. The more he worked the puck, the better he got. Suzette was in her own world, praying to God he didn't get killed. The other team sent over a couple men and the game started.

Victor didn't go out on the first shift. Moe scored a goal, as usual. But then the other team scored one, too. Joe had to do a double shift on defense. And then it happened. Joe hit Victor with a pass and the other team thought it was Moe: Victor was a burst of speed and left everybody behind and came up with a wrist shot in the corner of the net.

When they changed shifts again, the captain of the other team asked Moe, "Who the hell is that guy?"

"He's only the greatest figure skater in the world. That's Victor LaBuld."

"No shit. He supposed to be in the Olympics."

"He decided not to go. The competition wasn't good enough. He figured he'd come down and kick some hockey player's ass."

"You're just lucky, Moe, that this is a friendly game, or we'd put that figure skater right into the boards."

"You got to catch him first, right?"

After the game, Joe kept on Victor, "Why don't you sign up for spring league with us? If you aren't figure skating any more, you still got it in hockey."

Victor looked at Moe. "Why not? What do you think, Moe? Do I still have it?"

Moe's only remark was, "Shit!"

Victor got dressed and found Suzette in the lobby, waiting to scold him. "Are you crazy? You could have gotten hurt."

"Honey, you can't hurt a man whose destiny is already set. It was great."

Suzette saw the sparkle around him. The one thing she wasn't going to do was take anything away from her husband.

"You scored two goals!"

Victor grinned at her. "That's the good news. The bad news is that I'm going to skate with these guys in the spring league. And now let's get hopping. We're going to Rush St. with the guys."

Suzette went with him. She wanted him with her every minute because the time was so short. Yet, she knew she had to let life have its share of him and his share of it.

This time Victor had a pair of sunglasses with which to disguise himself. But there was no way he could conceal that handsome face. Once again he partook of the sixty second drill and was spotted by a reporter and cameraman who snapped pictures of an inebriated Victor LaBuld.

And once again, the next day Mary and William had to endure the cruel remarks at the restaurant. Mary's only recourse was to silently pray for her son and William, being a man, could weep only when he was alone. Even in Mokena, Sr. Richard read about her nephew and as she said her prayers in the chapel, wondered how he could change over night. She called Mary at the restaurant and asked her to tell Victor when he called to come and see her. Maybe she could help. Sr. Richard felt the hurt they were going through.

When Victor did call his mother, Mary scolded him at first. Having said her piece, she gently asked, "Victor, what's wrong?"

Victor handed over the phone to Suzette. Mary told her that Sr. Richard wanted Victor to call her. After Suzette hung up, she relayed the message. Adding, as usual, "Don't you think you should tell them?"

Always, Victor's reply was, "I love them."

Victor drove down to Sr. Richard without Suzette because he explained to her he had to do this by himself. When he arrived in Mokena, he waited for Sr. Richard to finish giving out the medications. Then Victor, Sr. Richard, and Sr. Bertha went out for lunch. Sr. Bertha talked on and on about Ada, with Sr. Richard joining the reminiscing.

131

When Sr. Bertha ordered lunch, she wistfully uttered, "Oh, I wish they had Limburger cheese on the menu."

"Why would you want that?" asked Victor.

"The cooks feed us well enough at the convent, but I have such a taste for Limburger. Oh well, no sense wishing for what you can't have."

Sr. Richard indulged her taste buds, "And wouldn't it taste good on sour dough rye bread or sauerkraut rye bread?"

The two nuns giggled like schoolgirls. Sr. Bertha continued the gourmet fantasy, "But it's been so long since we've had any. I guess the bakery must be out of business."

Sr. Richard added, "Yes, we all loved that bread. It was so good with a little pat of butter."

Sr. Richard had problems making up her mind: steak or Belgian waffle? They never had broiled steak at the convent - there were too many sisters to serve, and they never had big round waffles - only the square frozen kind. She didn't know which to order. Victor took care of the problem: he ordered both. Sr. Richard was overwhelmed by such wisdom, but there was no way she could eat that much food. The waitress didn't mind putting the leftovers into doggie bags.

After the meal, Victor drove the nuns back to the convent. Sr. Richard said, "Let's you and I visit the chapel."

As they sat in the chapel, Sr. Richard looked at Victor. "What's going on, young man?"

"What do you mean?"

"Victor, I've been on this planet too long to know that a nice young man like you shouldn't have so much bad publicity. First your Mother tells me you're quitting the Olympics and now I read you're out drinking."

"Stop, Sr. Richard. Don't say anymore. I need to tell you something, but I must have your word you won't tell anyone, especially Mom and Dad. I'm dying. I have cancer. I only have six to eighteen months to live. I'm not going to be a burden to anyone and I don't want anyone to feel sorry for me. God has written the script. And even though it hurt at first, why should I pity myself? I've learned from an old friend that young soldiers go to war and never see the world. I also know little children who have done no wrong in the world get hit by cars and die. God has reasons, Sister, and you don't ask Him why. All you ask is am I worthy of You?"

As he spoke, Sr. Richard clutched her rosary beads tighter and tighter. When he finished, she hugged him.

Then Victor added, "You know, I'm a lot like you and Sister Bertha. Instead of bread or cheese, the only thing I've really ever wanted was for my parents to see me skate. So, Sr. Richard, don't let the newspapers judge me, let God judge me. And in the end, you decide if you have a bad nephew."

On the drive home, Victor wondered, "These women ask for nothing and yet they give so much. Without medals, without glory. Sometimes without even a thank you."

How could Sr. Richard say she had a bad nephew? The next day he found a bakery - Dinkel's - that made just the right bread and brought eight loaves, and a delicatessen that sold Limburger cheese. He and Suzette took a little drive and dropped off the goodies at the convent. Sr. Richard shared the bread with all the sisters in the dining room. But no one wanted to share Sr. Bertha's Limburger cheese.

Two weeks had passed since Victor had seen Dr. King. He showed up for his first appointment and, just as Dr. King had said, Victor had the time slot preceding the Coach.

Dr. King examined Victor. The pain had been stabilized by medication. After the physical exam, Dr. King spoke to Victor. "How are you and the Coach doing?"

"He's a big help, Dr. King. Some of the things he says, no one in the world would understand. But when I think about them I realize how true they are. I don't understand why he won't go to an ice rink."

"Let me worry about that, Victor. You haven't been skating, have you?"

Victor hung his head and smiled. "I haven't been figure skating."

"I mean any kind of skating."

"Well, I did play a hockey game."

Dr. King threw his hands up in the air. "A hockey game! Victor, you shouldn't be on the ice for anything."

"Dr. King, I know I'm going to die. Would you rather have me stay in the house to brood and tell myself how rotten life is? Or should I use these last few months to live and make the best of it?"

"But hockey? There's an old man sitting out there who's loaded with scars and broken bones. Hockey is fun?"

Victor smiled. "I know another old man who would give anything to even see a hockey game."

Dr. King knew who he was talking about.

"Doctor, in a couple of weeks, I want to take a trip to Europe with my wife. I owe her."

"Victor, you don't owe anybody."

"She's going to have my baby who if I'm lucky, I might get to see for a few months. I want to give her some happy memories. I do owe her that. I'm going to take her to Europe. Do you see any problem with that?"

Dr. King realized Victor was going to do it with or without his blessing. He put his hand on Victor's shoulder and smiling said, "Just stay out of hockey games."

When Victor finished, it was the Coach's turn to see the doctor. The Coach said, "Stick around, kid. We'll have some coffee when I'm done."

After the Coach was finished, he had Victor follow him in his car. Victor suddenly realized where he was - Damen and Roscoe. They parked and went into the Lucky Lady. At the bar, everybody knew the Coach, but they called him Jr.

"You know, my father used to be across the street selling hot dogs and newspapers, don't you, Coach?"

"I told you before this is the place I wrote the poem about the dog."

Just then a fight broke out in the back. Victor thought how this bar matched the Coach's personality - one of the roughest in the city.

"You know, Victor, I used to sit here wishing I could go across the street and say hi. I remember one night when I went across the street to deal with a couple of drunks who were harassing those blind men. The drunks scattered after I told them if I ever caught them by that stand again I'd tear their hearts out."

"Why couldn't you say hello to my Father?"

"Your Father and Ed are special. They're heroes to the world. The people who buy the hot dogs from them think they're doing them a favor. If they only knew the true story of how your Dad and Ed lost their eyes in a war. You see, that's why Vietnam to me was so easy. There's right and there's wrong, but there's no in-between. In Special Forces you walk and make no sound. You kill without blinking an eye. You throw away the Bible. That's God's Book. But you never throw away God. You want your country to pin medals on you and honor you as a hero. But to do that, you have to take the dirtiest jobs. You do them and do them well. So well that you become immune to what you're doing. I loved the jungle. That's the difference between your Father and me. They didn't like what they were doing. But you see, I threw away God's Book and I forgot that He published more than one. When I picked It up again, I realized what I was. But He's a forgiving God. All you young men are the ones getting me to heaven." The Coach smiled at Victor. "You know you're one of those kids, don't you? The only thing is He must have gotten mad at me again. I had an accident and fell from a beam. And He won't let those nightmares from Vietnam go away. But whatever the next project He gives me, I'll give Him my best shot. And kid, there's nothing I wouldn't do for a brother soldier."

"You mean like my Dad, Coach?"

"Your Dad, your Uncle Ed."

"Does that pertain to their kids?"

"Of course it does."

"Then I want to ask you for a favor."

After a few days Victor and Suzette went to see his parents. Victor broke the news about their going to Europe and France to see the Olympics.

Finally for the first time in his life, William burst out at his son. "You know, Victor, I never quit in anything in all my life, although I was close. I never thought you would quit."

"I'm not as tough as you, Dad. I just had enough of figure skating and that's it. Can you understand that?"

"Tell your Grandma that and see what she would say."

Victor saw his father's hurt and ended the conversation by leaving. Suzette was on the verge of tears as she thought, "If they only knew."

Victor and Suzette arrived in France in time for the figure skating finals. At the arena he wore his sunglasses, but Victor was only fooling himself. People, along with reporters, recognized him in the stands. As the competition went on, he paid no attention to them. Victor smiled as he watched his colleagues perform. It didn't matter which country or sex they were. He applauded each one. Suzette had to show her strength as she watched her husband cheer those who had fulfilled their dreams.

Back in Chicago, Ed had the TV going in the bar. The regular patrons didn't say a word about Victor. But as usual, there was a drunk waiting to make a stupid statement. "It's a shame the United States has a coward who can't take the pressure. All those figure skaters are the same way. Spoiled little brats. More worried about their publicity and if their hair is combed. That Victor LaBuld really let down his country."

Mary Jo walked over to the drunk. "If you don't keep your thoughts to yourself, sir, you can leave the bar."

"And who do you think you are?"

"I'm the woman who's going to kick your ass out the door. As a matter of fact, out!"

The man muttered, "I got a better place than this to drink in."

Between performances, the cameras panned the audience and caught Victor, Suzette, and Miss Rubin. Just like the drunk, the sportscasters considered Victor fair game for their cruel comments.

William hid himself in the kitchen with his wife and Ian where they could still hear the familiar ice rink music from the TV.

William scrubbed the pots and pans until they were shinier than when they were new.

Mary in her mind replayed the thought, "What did we do wrong?"

The worst thoughts came from Mary Jo thinking how could her daughter have married such a cruel man. But since she herself hadn't gotten a call either, perhaps they deserved each other.

CHAPTER EIGHT

After the awarding of the medals, Victor and Suzette took Miss Rubin out to dinner. Just like Suzette, Miss Rubin thought to herself as she sat at the table, "How courageous of Victor, trying to hide his pain and give no pain to those he loves."

"Miss Rubin, I have a favor to ask you."

"Anything, Victor, just name it."

"I want to give one more performance."

"But what about your health?"

"Does it matter? The world thinks I'm a coward. Even my Dad thinks I'm a coward."

"The only reason he thinks that is because you haven't told him the truth."

"Who cares about the world? It's not the world I'm worried about. It's the sport. You know what they say about us: everything is given to us, we've never worked a day in our lives. I'd just like to see one of those reporters do a simple waltz jump. I know we didn't win because of my health. I know all the time you've invested in me. Now, I ask you, let me go out as a winner. I've got one other person that said he'd help me on the ice. But before I can say who he is I want you to give me a yes or no."

"You know the answer's yes. Who's the other person?"

Victor smiled. "Coach Wolf."

"He's dead."

"No, Miss Rubin, he's still alive."

"Oh shit."

The rest of the night, the conversation centered on the Coach and the hockey team. Suzette told her about the sixty second drills and adult men who needed diapers.

The next day Miss Rubin returned to the States to set up ice times for practice. She looked up an old acquaintance, Albert Hoffman, who was in town to negotiate the contract for an ice show at the Stadium. He was glad to see her, but hesitant to sign Victor LaBuld to a one-night performance because of his

139

reputation as a quitter. She made Al promise not to reveal the secret. She concluded the explanation with an assurance of tons of favorable publicity after his performance. Al understood and agreed to the contract.

Victor and Suzette spent a couple weeks in France, then went on to Israel. They toured all the historic sites and when they arrived in Jericho, the guide described its historical importance.

Victor added, "This country is so full of miracles. Jesus gave sight to the blind, made the lame walk, rose Lazarus from the dead. It would be great if He were still alive and could perform a miracle for my parents."

"How do you know so much about the Bible?"

"I went to St. Benedict's, didn't I? I was also raised by God-loving people." Then Victor began laughing. "I've got it. I know who the Coach was."

Suzette looked queerly at Victor. "The Coach is the Coach."

"No, he was Samson. He told the world to blind him, to give them an advantage. But he still kicked their ass!" Victor continued laughing as they toured the ruins.

The blind continued their everyday life. The Olympics faded from their mind. Victor LaBuld was no longer discussed as the should-have-been. More serious events were taking place. At the bar, Ed had a yuppie know-it-all stop in nearly every day for a drink. He enjoyed putting down those in the bar who weren't college graduates. He had an answer for everything.

Ed's brain had conceived the ultimate in humiliation for the yuppie. On a day when the yuppie didn't put in an appearance, Mary Jo taped an episode of "Jeopardy." Three weeks later, Ed replayed it as though it were that day's program. But Ed had done his homework: he knew every question.

Mary Jo worked the bar this day so Ed could sit next to the yuppie. When the previously recorded "Jeopardy" aired, Mary Jo egged on the yuppie for the answers, and when he didn't know them, Ed stepped in to the rescue. The other customers' attention turned to the match. Ed won "Final Jeopardy" by a landslide and the entire bar applauded Ed as the yuppie silently, humbly finished his drink, exited, and never was seen there again.

Mel got the biggest charge out of this when he heard about it at the weekly card game. He asked his partners if they wanted to go to Rush St. to cause a little mischief. He was ready for a little glory in life. He wanted to show his friends he had a mind as devious as Ed's, but they had to keep it secret from the ladies.

Mel wore sunglasses and used a cane. On Rush St. the four blind mice converged on a strip joint. If Mel hadn't been a lawyer, he should have been an actor. Every time the audience hooted and hollered their approval, Mel, followed by the others in his group, booed. The blind men's remarks became so lewd that the strippers complained to the owners to have the four men removed. The owner and two bouncers told the group to leave. Ian explained that they had their civil rights while Mel explained the law to them, especially freedom of speech. Ed got in the picture by threatening a countersuit - the girls were ugly and fat and the place was a rip-off. William agreed with him. The owner had enough. "Blind" or not, the bouncers escorted them out. As they were being unceremoniously kicked out, Eddie drove by in his squad car and couldn't believe who he saw. He parked and with his partner walked over to the commotion. "What's the problem here?"

"These four men were starting trouble in my place."

Eddie looked at the men and hid his amusement. "You mean, these four blind men are causing a problem?"

"Don't let those glasses and canes fool you. Most of my customers try to disguise themselves."

Ed recognized the voice of the officer. He knew he could now get away with murder. "Officer, we just came here, looking for my wife. She was kidnaped two weeks ago. We heard she was in this promiscuous joint." Mel pointed at Ian, "And his grandmother, too."

The owner was dumbfounded. He couldn't believe his eyes when all the men took off their glasses and Mel winked at him.

Two little old ladies passing by thought the police department was so sweet because the officers loaded the four blind men into their squad car to take them home.

The next day at the office, Mel enjoyed telling and retelling his adventure. June and Willis were miffed that the men referred to June and Willis's grandmother as hookers.

Life had resumed it normal routine and the absence of Victor and Suzette, though not approved of, was at least tolerated.

Everyone tried to take William's mind off Victor. Despite all the pranks and practical jokes, William couldn't stop thinking of his son. At home, Mary went into his room, grasped his trophies as tears streamed down her cheeks. Misty's favorite spot was Victor's bed as though sleeping on it brought back memories of days long gone.

One night in late May, June phoned them. "Mary, I just read in the paper that Victor's going to star in one special performance in the ice show."

"Oh June, enough of the gags. That's not very funny."

"Mary, I swear it's true. Victor is starring in one performance."

"That must mean they're back from Europe."

"I don't know. They might be practicing over there. It would be thoughtful if those kids would call you once in a while and let you know what's going on. Oh Mary, I'm sorry. I didn't mean to hurt you or William. You've had enough pain."

"That's alright, June. We're all under a lot of stress. Let me hang up and tell William what's going on."

Mary excitedly blurted out the news to him, but William remained expressionless, as passive as stone. He finally spoke, "Mary, I really don't care. That boy has changed so much. I just don't understand it. They say money is the root of all evil. Well, maybe that's true. In this year since Miss Rockwell died, Victor had all the money and fame anyone could want. But he's thrown away his family and even skating. We have a grandchild on the way and we don't even know how Suzette and the baby are doing. Living it up in Europe, never calling, not even caring

142

about all of us who love him. Is he ashamed of us because we're blind? Or because we work in the restaurant? I thought we raised him better than that. Mary, I can't take the hurt any more. I don't want to hear his name again. I had you before I had Victor. I will take care of you, Mary. I won't let our son hurt you any longer."

The restaurant was buzzing with the news of Victor's performance. Yet, William turned a deaf ear to it all. Mary stayed in the kitchen where she insulated herself from it.

Mary Jo spoke with Ian. "I don't understand any of this. My own daughter can't call her Mother and say howd'ye-do. That grandbaby may already be born and no one knows anything. I would have been the best grandma on this earth. But that's their loss. I tried calling, but their phone's disconnected. I've tried to be a good mother - I gave her all my love even if I couldn't give her everything the other kids had. I worked a second job for her figure skating. These kids nowadays are spoiled brats who think only of themselves. I guess a mom who's just a waitress isn't glamorous enough for her. But she'll get hers. What goes around, comes around."

As Ian grabbed her hand, he tried to console her. "Mary Jo, even our Lord asked for forgiveness for those who crucified him. 'Forgive them, Father, for they know not what they do.' Can't you find it in your heart to forgive them?"

Mary Jo's only response was a flood of tears.

The road we call Life has many twists and turns. Mary and William were detoured by depression and despair when the route ahead showed signs of hope. Mary received a phone call from another lawyer, Martin Fiedler who repeated a message similar to Mr. Jonscher's, but money was not involved. A donation by a woman who had only one or two weeks to live had been made to them based on magazine articles she'd read. Because this woman loved figure skating so much, she wanted to make it possible for both of them to see Victor's performance. Mr. Fiedler set up an appointment for them to see him immediately.

June drove them to Mr. Fiedler's office where he explained more fully the donation. "The anonymous lady has leukemia and in less than two weeks will die. But her eyes are unaffected. She has made the financial and medical arrangements to enable each of you to undergo an eye transplant."

William recalled, "Mr. Fiedler, once a very generous woman left my son a sizable inheritance. We received a great deal of money also. We have seen how it has destroyed our son and our family's happiness. I don't want my wife to endure any more pain because of outsiders' well-meant generosity."

Mr. Fiedler said, "This is a one-shot deal. Money can't buy this. I don't want to pressure you, but time is very short."

They were skeptical. Mr. Fiedler supplied more details, everything except the name of the donor. He also outlined the risks involved and the possibility that it might not be successful. Dr. Horn, the noted eye surgeon would perform the surgery.

William broke the silence. "Mary, what if it didn't work? Would you be able to live with that? The let down might be too much for you to bear."

"Just think, William, if only I could see for five minutes, I'd know what a tree looked like. I'd know what my family and friends looked like. I'd know what you looked like. And I could keep that memory always."

Finally William reconsidered. "I would like to be able to see again. But it's not to see Victor skate. It's not for my son in any way. I've never seen what my wife looks like. I'd love to see her face each morning when we wake up."

Mary remained quiet, but her feelings had been expressed by her husband.

June sat silently through the discussions. As they left, she quietly added, "I think you should both do it."

Two days later, William and Mary checked into the hospital. Both were hesitant, unsure of their journey's outcome.

Dr. Horn had each patient assigned a private room, in case one of the operations was not successful. Mary and William had thought they would be in the same room. Dr. Horn soothed their fears.

144

During the pre-op tests, Mary and William each thought the same thoughts - how the other person would enjoy seeing. William especially wanted his wife to enjoy the gift of sight: to see what she had only felt or had had described to her. Mary wanted William to have restored what had been taken from him so long ago. Each playfully wondered what the other looked like. Mary had a wonderful image of the man she loved, but his physical appearance would never change her love and commitment to him. At the same time he wondered what she looked like. Mary remembered William saying how money had caused them so much tragedy. She prayed that this chance to see would not have tragic consequences.

That evening as William sat on Mary's bed, their thoughts centered on Victor, but neither expressed them.

The phone rang. Mary answered it and recognized the voice. "Hi, Mom, I've heard the news. Boy I hope everything goes alright. If it does, Mom, maybe you and Dad can watch me skate at the Stadium when I come into town. Things have been really hectic. The rehearsals are time-consuming. Suzette had a baby boy. I just couldn't get away to come to the hospital, but I know everything will be okay."

"Your Father is sitting next to me. Would you like to talk to him?"

"I really don't have the time. I have to get back on the ice. Tell him I love him and his son was never a quitter."

Mary hung up the phone.

"You don't have to tell me who it was. I know. How is he?"

"He's skating and getting ready for the show."

"I don't care about myself, Mary, but I think he should have been here for you."

"William, let's not think about it. Let's just think about you and me. We have a new grandson."

"I hope he doesn't turn out like our son."

"Let's concentrate on a miracle."

When William left to return to his room down the hall, both thought about Sr. Richard and hoped that her prayers would help them face what loomed on the horizon.

They awoke early the next morning and were prepped for the operation. As they laid in the operating room, dimly aware of the noises, Mary spoke to William through the drowsiness, "William, I feel so alone. Whatever happens, William, I love you."

"I love you, too, Mary."

Then William broke down, "I wish our son were here. Even if your Aunt were here - she's so close to God. We need Him on our side"

Both drifted into a silent sleep.

The first to wake up was Mary. She felt a burning sensation in her bandaged eyes. Through the pain she whispered, "William, are you there?"

"No, Mary, he's still sedated. He's just coming out of it." She recognized Sr. Richard's voice.

"Sr. Richard, is that you?"

"Yes, Mary, I'm here. William's still pretty groggy."

"Is he alright?"

"He's fine, Mary. Are you alright?"

"My head hurts, but I'll survive. Are you sure William's okay?"

"Mary, there's an angel protecting the both of you."

"What did the doctor say?"

"Mary, you're not going to know for a few weeks. But Dr. Horn said the surgery went well."

As William was coming out of the anesthesia, he called out, "Mary, are you there? Are you alright?" It seemed they both had one track minds.

A nurse came, ready to wheel Mary to her room. Mary insisted she didn't want to leave her husband, but Sr. Richard convinced her it was alright. They both needed to rest.

Thank God for Mary Jo, June, and Sr. Richard. The three women took turns being at the hospital over the next two weeks. They wheeled Mary to Williams' room and William to Mary's room. It was difficult keeping them apart.

146

One day Mary said June, "I want to ask you a question and I want to know the truth."

"What is it?"

"I know I've asked you this before, but it's more important than ever now. Am I really pretty? Please tell me the truth."

"Mary, why are you worrying about this? Of course, you're a pretty woman."

"Well, now there's that chance that William might see what I really look like, and if I'm not pretty, maybe he won't love me as much."

"William would love you no matter what. He loves you because you're Mary."

Dr. Horn knew when the day came for removing the bandages, it would be a major upset if one or the other or both couldn't see. He not only had to be a surgeon, but also a psychiatrist.

William was the first to have his removed. He laid in bed praying to God to answer his prayers. Doctor Horn told him to open his eyes slowly. As he did so, William still saw darkness and blurry shadows. As the nurse started opening the blinds, William realized he could see - not clearly, but slowly the faces became clearer and clearer. Then William let out a loud yell, "I can see again! I can see."

Dr. Horn looked down at William's ear to ear smile. He proceeded to tell William how his vision would improve as each day went by, and the instructions as to what to do and what not to do. "Well, William, I think I'll leave you alone to rest for a while. I'd like to go and see you wife now."

As Dr. Horn left William's room, he was pleased that the job had been well done. He entered Mary's room with the nurse. "Good morning, Mary."

"Is this the day, doctor?"

"Yes, it is, Mary."

"Did you take care of my husband?"

He fibbed a little. "I'll get to him later." He didn't want to upset her in case her results weren't as favorable.

147

She kept asking how William was. Finally, Dr. Horn asked, "Do you think you're ready to begin?"

"Yes, I think so. I'm just a little bit frightened, though."

"Of course you are," said the doctor as he patted her on the shoulder. He called for the nurse to assist him in the removal of the bandages. To Mary it seemed to take forever. Finally Dr. Horn told her to open her eyes slowly. Everything was dark, but as she slowly opened her eyes, she saw blurred visions and shadows emerging from the darkness. Things were becoming clearer and clearer.

The nurse opened the blinds a little and then Mary said, "Dr. Horn, I'm almost afraid to believe this, but I'm sure I can see things."

"Take your time, Mary. Don't overtax yourself. Just do it slowly."

"Oh my God! Dr. Horn, is that you?" she asked as she held out her hand towards the doctor.

"It's me," he said as he held out his hand and grasped Mary's. Then he moved his hand away and Mary moved her hand to follow his and grabbed on to it.

"I can see. It's really true! Oh my God in heaven, thank you for this miracle. Thank you."

Mary was about to cry. Dr. Horn quickly cautioned her, "Please, Mary, don't cry. Your eyes are so sensitive right now. You still need a lot of rest."

"What about William?"

"We'll tend to William, Mary. Let's see if you can rest a little now."

"But there's so many things I want to look at."

"There's plenty of time for that. Your eyes will be under severe strain for quite some time and be extremely sensitive. You must take it slow and easy. I don't want you getting out of bed for a day or so." Dr. Horn smiled and so did Mary.

"I can see my own hands. I can see parts of my own body. I can see colors. I don't know which color is which, but it's so wonderful."

"Yes, Mary, it is wonderful, but I'd like you to rest now and put on this eye mask. I'll be back later to remove it for a while."

"Alright, Dr. Horn, whatever you say. But before you go would you do me a favor?"

"If I can."

"I'd like to see a mirror."

He handed her one from the side table. Mary held it up to her face. She stared and stared. She wanted to see if she was really pretty, but then she realized how would she know what pretty was and what it wasn't. Everything was beautiful to her at that moment.

The doctor and nurse left Mary to rest.

As Mary laid in the dimly lit room, her mind remained on William. She remembered the phone and dialed the room number. It rang and rang. William didn't answer. Mary panicked. He must have had something go wrong. She didn't care what Dr. Horn said. She got out of bed, removed the eye mask and for the first time, without her cane, maneuvered herself out the door and down the hall, squinting as she went. She had to ask the volunteer selling newspapers where room 409 was. Mary didn't know how to read the room numbers, she only knew Braille.

When she got to his room, she looked at William's empty bed. Where was he? She knew something had happened. She let out a scream. Pandemonium ensued. Every nurse ran into the room. "What are you doing out of bed, Mary?" one of the nurses asked.

"Where is my husband?"

Then they realized, where was William?

One of the nurses went into the hallway and called out, "William LaBuld, where are you? Get your butt back here. You're not supposed to be out of bed."

William yelled back, "I'm looking for my wife."

One of the nurses ran to him. "William, you must come back to your room."

"I'm not going back to my room until I see my wife."

The nurse smiled. "William, you just passed her in the hall!"

Mary was told the same thing.

To calm them down, the nurses let them look at each other for the first time. Not one nurse had dry eyes.

William and Mary hugged each other and looked into each other's eyes. Mary caressed William's face as she told him, "I love you, William. Can you see?"

He reassured her as he held her closely. "Yes, Mary, I can. How about you?"

"It's a strange, wonderful world. I don't know what's ugly or handsome. But it doesn't matter. You'll always be my knight. All I know is I don't think I could ever live without you."

The nurses had to get their patients back into their beds. The head nurse said, "Well, I can see that the best thing to do for you two is to have you both in the same room. I don't see any sense in waiting until tomorrow."

At the nurses station, everyone was chattering about the bond of love so evident between William and Mary. They were as in love as newlyweds.

William was moved into Mary's room. As they laid in their beds, they disobeyed the doctor's orders and stared at each other.

William said, "I didn't know I married such a beautiful woman."

"You must be handsome, William, because June told me you were. June said you had black hair. I don't understand something. I don't know my colors, but you seem to have two colors of hair."

William cracked up. "Mary, I have gotten older and when you get older, your hair changes to gray."

Mary knew that as people got older their hair changed, but she never felt she and William aged because the darkness had never let her see time.

Just then Ed and June walked into the room. "Well, how are you two doing?" June asked.

Right away Mary and William knew who June was from her voice.

"June and Ed," Mary said, "we can see. Both of us can see."

"I know. Ed and I talked to the doctor before we came up. We can't tell you how happy we are."

They all embraced each other.

150

And then Ed, always the comic, said, "Well, now, the two of you can keep an eye out for each other."

It was funny, and then again it wasn't. "Poor Ed," William and Mary thought, "if only he could have had the same chance as we had. Maybe someday, he'll get a break like this. Maybe there's a miracle for him, too."

A nurse came in and said they had to rest. It had been too much for one day.

For the rest of their hospital stay, William answered Mary's questions and realized how much he'd have to teach her. William and Mary's vision improved day by day.

When they finally came home, Mary started wearing pajamas to bed at night. Now that her husband could see her, she caught him staring at her and felt embarrassed. Those weeks that passed were filled with excitement and enjoyment for Mary. She was curious about everything. Just going shopping for groceries was a big event. William was right there alongside her to teach and reassure her about everything she needed to know.

William and Mary took a vacation from the restaurant. They'd never known a honeymoon, except for Morristown. William was going to make sure his wife got to see everything in the city of Chicago. The only thing they didn't see was their son or grandson. That thought haunted them.

Misty could now retire as a working dog. Although it was debatable as to whether she was one or a food disposal. Misty sensed the change in her owners, but the emptiness caused by Victor's absence never diminished.

The day before Victor's performance had arrived. Mary and William were at the restaurant - as customers on their vacation - when Sr. Richard dropped in. "Mary, I just got these tickets from Victor in the mail. He'd like all his family and friends to see him tomorrow night."

These words brought to the surface all the hurt and pain Mary silently had harbored. "Where was he when we needed him? Not even a phone call since we've been out of the hospital. Is he so desperate for an audience that he has to give away tickets? The only time he knows us is when he wants us to pay homage to him? No, thank you, Sr. Richard. We don't need that kind of son."

William and the rest of the family felt the same way.

"I see now we haven't been listening in church for a long time. I see that we haven't read the Bible lately. We all must be perfect here." The words stung Mary's heart. Sr. Richard continued, "I wonder what Ada would think. I know she would go and see Victor, probably using that old movie camera to capture his entire routine. I guess Victor was born bad. Maybe after his performance they should lock him up and throw away the key. He's such a bad kid."

William looked at Sr. Richard and shook his head. Did she detect the hint of a smile? "I remember what you said one time, Sister, about the man who had no shoes and complained until he saw the man with no feet. We do have a son."

Mary Jo enter the conversation. "Maybe our grandson will be there. That's the only reason I'd go."

After she distributed the tickets, as was her custom, Sr. Richard hugged and kissed each one and knew she would say a special prayer in the chapel that the family would understand and forgive Victor's behavior.

The next evening at the Stadium, William and Mary were impressed by the number of people coming to see Victor. The family was seated in their own section, the entire front row was reserved for them. Everyone was there: Mel and Connie; Eddie and Tommy; Ian, Willis, and John; and June and Ed. Ed made sure he got Misty in by harnessing her as his guide dog. Misty didn't mind at all. Ed kept bribing her with beer and hot dogs.

The group saw Sr. Bertha and Sr. Richard approaching. Sr. Richard was holding a baby. "Suzette asked me if we could watch the baby. She has to sit with a band of angels." She placed Victor LaBuld II in his Grandpa's waiting arms. He was dressed in a little hockey uniform, a replica of Victor's down to the 27 on his back. William was overwhelmed by a feeling that his son was trying to tell him something. But what was it?

Both Grandmas were sitting, drooling, waiting for their chance to hold the baby. As much as Mary cared about Mary Jo and vice versa, they both wanted to hold the baby next. William politely gave him to Mary Jo. All the negative thoughts towards Victor and Suzette fled when the baby smiled. When Mary Jo gave him to Mary, they heard from the other side of the rink a commotion by a motley group - tousled hair, black eyes, broken noses, missing teeth. Although dressed in suits there was no way they'd be considered angels. Suzette was seated in the midst of them. As they looked further, they saw Miss Rubin and an unknown man, Dr. King, near the performers' waiting area.

The lights dimmed. The show began. For the next forty-five minutes the skaters performed. There was comedy, couples skating, and the usual number with the entire troupe participating. Soon it was intermission and after the ice machine had cleaned the ice and the water hardened, the noisy crowd began to quiet down.

The final act was Victor's. The Stadium was in complete darkness, then a spotlight hit the center of the ice. There was Victor dressed in a black tux, exactly like the first outfit he'd ever worn. He was still wearing sunglasses disguising himself from the media. The crowd began screaming and yelling, whistling and applauding like nothing they'd done earlier. Once again the silence fell. The music of "Malaguena" began. How many times had William and Mary heard this song, but now they saw how their son skated to every beat of the music. Everything Victor did the crowd applauded. Mary and William were amazed at how great Victor was. The tears were welling up in their eyes. Victor executed a triple and the glare from the spotlight caught Moe's clenched fist raised above his head in a salute to Victor as Moe shouted, "Yes!" The performance was truly beautiful. Every time Victor performed a jump or spiral, his shadow showed two of him. The hockey players sat in astonishment. Up near the top rafter, a grubby, army-jacketed man studied the proceedings. He was too shabby, unshaven, and reeking of alcohol to be employed there. The man's intensity as he watched was not that of the casual observer. His fists clutched tightly in anticipation of every move, as though he had memorized the routine.

When the music was over, the audience stood and applauded for what seemed minutes. As Victor took his bows the applause grew louder and louder. The crowd knew they had seen perhaps the greatest figure skater in the world. The tears streamed down Mary and William's faces as they realized their dreams had been fulfilled. Their anger and hurt evaporated and love shone brighter than any star. Victor's grace and agility let them soar to the top of the rainbow.

The spotlight followed Victor around the rink. He paused where his parents were sitting just long enough to hug them and say, "I love you." Misty caught sight of him and went crazy trying to get to her playmate on the ice. If it weren't for her weight problem, she would have leaped over the boards in a single bound.

As he was skating off the ice, Victor fell. The lights went on. He laid there until Dr. King and Miss Rubin helped him off the ice and to his dressing room.

William and Mary had to fight their way through the crowd, explaining on the way that they were his parents. Sr. Richard and the security guards helped and led them to Victor's dressing room. As soon as they entered they saw Suzette already there.

Victor was lying on the floor as Dr. King worked on him. An ambulance had already been called.

Mary and William were in hysteria. "What's wrong with our son?"

Dr. King looked up at them, but the answer shown on his face. "I'm sorry. Victor's dead."

"No, no, he can't be," cried Mary.

"I'm his doctor."

Then William spoke, "Who says you're his doctor?"

Mary Jo arrived just as Sr. Richard began, "William, Mary, Mary Jo. This is Dr. King. He's been treating Victor for cancer."

"Cancer! What are you talking about? Victor just skated his greatest performance." Mary sobbed.

Mary Jo walked to her daughter and hugged her. "I think you're more of a woman than I could ever be."

Suzette said, "It took a woman to raise a woman."

Then Suzette took over. She reached down to her husband and removed his sunglasses. They could see his glass eyes.

Everyone was shocked.

"Both my Moms, Dad, Victor knew he had only a few more weeks to live." Suzette was crying and smiling as she continued. "When you got the phone call in the hospital from Victor and you thought he was practicing, he was really down the hall from you. Each night he stopped in and checked on you. You said on the operating table, Dad, that you wished your son was there. You do not know how hard it was to remain silent then. I was in the room with Victor. He wanted you and Mom to have his eyes if it were possible. Victor knew if he told you he had cancer, you would have felt the pain with him. He knew God had given you enough pain in your life. He knew you would never have accepted his eyes.

"Don't be angry with the people who helped keep the secret. Dr. King kept the pain from Victor. Although he didn't want to go along with it, he couldn't deny Victor his request. He recommended Dr. Horn to perform the surgery.

"Sr. Richard, Victor knew by your prayers that God would find the strength for him to climb a building higher than the Sears Tower.

"Miss Rubin, you've stuck with my husband all the way through this. He considered you one of the greatest teachers that ever lived. He also thought of you as a close friend. At night we'd laugh and chuckle knowing you had to work with the Coach."

William and Mary mumbled to themselves, "The Coach?"

Miss Rubin looked at them. "Yes, that old buzzard bait is still alive."

Dr. King was amused by their reaction to that tidbit.

Suzette continued, "The Coach is the one who taught Victor to skate blindfolded, almost like a cat.

"Dad, Victor wanted me to tell you this. If he was never a skater, he thought he could have been a good soldier. He even thought he could have been in Special Forces. He figured if he could withstand the Coach's punishment, he could have done anything. As strange as the Coach is, he gave Victor the courage to understand about Life.

"Dad, you and Uncle Ed are as close as any two men could be. But these last few months, Victor and Moe developed that same bond of togetherness and friendship. Along the way, they let me join them. I used to think hockey players were the crudest, most uncouth animals in the world. But I discovered they're only angels - with black eyes."

Facing Mary, Suzette went on. "Mom, do not believe the newspapers. They make up their stories sometimes. I think they should themselves be judged instead of being judges.

"We were planning on a party, but Victor always told me if he didn't make it, to have the party anyway. This was one of his requests."

June, Ed, and the rest of the family arrived at the dressing room. Misty broke free from Ed and ran to Victor's side and laid down beside him.

The wail of the ambulance siren drew nearer. When the attendants approached Victor, for the first time in her life, Misty growled and threatened them. William soothed her enough so the men could carry out Victor's body.

Dr. King explained to everyone that there was nothing more that could be done. He suggested they go home.

The media was waiting for news of Victor. Miss Rubin issued a statement that Victor had just passed away.

No one slept that night. Mary Jo, Suzette, and the baby stayed with William and Mary. As they sat and talked, the pain was eased by remembering Victor's love. Mary wouldn't let go of the baby as she reminisced how she held Victor on her lap many years ago.

Suzette started giggling. "Do you know, Dad, one of the things Victor really wanted to do? He wanted to be in a hockey fight. Well, you should have seen him the night they kicked his

156

butt. When we patched him up, he was actually smiling about it. He said, 'Now I know what my Dad went through.'"

She told him how Victor drank so much in the sixty second drill that he ended up with diarrhea the next morning.

"Dad, we finally found out why the Coach called Grandma Miss Ogdensburg. It's where his grandparents are laid to rest. Victor saw the Wolf mausoleum at Grandma's funeral. And Grandma always thought it was her good looks and powers of persuasion that got Victor accepted in the clinic."

This produced the first glimmer of a smile on William's face.

Then Suzette explained how Victor treated her like a princess in Europe. She thought she had seen the greatest couple in William and Mary. "But, Dad and Mom, you're going to have to move over. Victor was just as great."

Mary stopped rocking the baby. "I think my son had the greatest wife." Mary looked at Suzette. "I think you're the hockey player. You're the tough one in this family."

"I cried every night, Mom. I never let Victor see me."

Finally they managed a few hours sleep.

The next day, Suzette made the funeral arrangements.

At the wake Mary and William could not believe how many friends Victor had. The restaurant was closed for the next few days so all the partners could lend their support to the grieving family.

Victor laid peacefully in the casket. His smile never left his face. Misty maintained her vigil next to the casket, sniffing her approval of the mourners. Her ears perked up. As everyone's attention focused on the lobby, a bunch of suited young men were ganging up on a foul smelling, but suited, old man. One of the young men walked up to Suzette who began smiling as he hugged her. "I'm Moe," he said as he extended his hand to William.

William squeezed his hand a little tighter and gave him a hug. This was William's first recognition of Moe. Mary also embraced him.

The other angels with black eyes approached William and Mary. They explained they were Victor's hockey teammates. When Joe Wood came to William, he said, "Your son was the greatest hockey player I've ever seen - besides Moe." A tear rolled down William's cheek.

Sr. Richard sat in a chair looking at the group of thugs. Generally a nun knows what a group of angels should look like, but she wasn't too sure about this group. She hoped St. Peter had a good plastic surgeon on call.

Mary Jo was seated next to Sr. Richard holding the baby. Each young man came up to the baby and grabbed his little fist. They said they knew he'd be as great a hockey player as his daddy had been.

Miss Rubin, on the other side of Mary Jo, watched and warned them, "You be gentle with that baby. Your hands better be clean if you touch my Godson."

They knew they'd better obey or else. Each responded, "Yes, ma'am."

A couple muttered, "She's worse than the Coach."

If they didn't obey the Godmother, the Godfather - Moe - would take care of them.

There was only one threat to Miss Rubin's dreams of working with another figure skater. She'd have to challenge these hockey players.

Suzette smiled as she saw a huge man enter. She hugged him and introduced the Coach. William grasped his hand and tightly shook it. "My mother and son greatly admired you, but I think I respect you even more."

Mary stared intently and knew what Ada meant - his breath was appalling although he was rather appealing when he was all dressed up. His eyes frightened her. They looked as if they had seen more than his share of tragedy.

The Coach gently said to her, "He's with the angels now. No more suffering. No more pain. He can skate with the great ones. You, Mary, haven't changed in all these years. You're still the prettiest woman on this earth, besides your mother-in-law."

Mary hugged the Coach and smiled. "I never saw you before. But you're as handsome as Ada said you were. It must be that water from Ogdensburg." In the back of her mind, she knew the Coach would have to mix that water with a lot of alcohol before he would drink it.

Even though William and Mary could see, it seemed like the same old disappearing act by the Coach. Silently they saw him kneeling at the casket. Misty hadn't moved the entire time, until now. She placed her head on the Coach's knee.

During the wake, Suzette told the mourners that the funeral luncheon would be at the restaurant. She didn't merely mention it, she strongly insisted they attend. So following the burial, the entire procession headed to the restaurant. All except the Coach who after the funeral retreated to his island.

When they entered the restaurant, they were astonished to see a big-screen television with VCR along one wall. Suzette explained this was part of Victor's last wishes. He didn't want a morbid luncheon. He wanted his family and friends to celebrate his realization of his dreams and happiness. They had compiled a special tape of Victor skating, both hockey and figure skating.

As she tapped her father-in-law on the shoulder, Suzette said, "Dad, you're really going to love this tape. Let me put it this way: the Coach told me this was the greatest line in hockey that anybody could have assembled."

Suzette pressed Play. William and Mary saw their son in a hockey uniform and Moe on the other side passing with precision to each other. It seemed as though everyone else on the ice stood still as the two speed demons, Moe and Victor, passed them. As William watched, he couldn't believe his son was that good. Figure skating? Yes. But hockey, too? Watching Moe with his son was a work of art no artist could create.

The film captured Victor at his best. When he scored a goal, both Victor and Moe did waltz jumps in front of the goalie to antagonize him. When Moe scored, they did spirals and lunges. Each goal infuriated not only the goalie, but also the rest of the opposing team. Fights abounded.

Mary gasped as she saw her son viciously man-handled. Then she realized in every altercation, Moe didn't allow him to be overly brutalized. He was Victor's guardian angel and big brother who stepped in to protect him when the going got too rough.

All Sr. Richard did was make the sign of the cross and whisper a quick prayer.

The on-lookers were amazed at Suzette's amount of profanity. As she taped the games and fights, her little comments were picked up by the camcorder. Everyone heard, "Kick that asshole's butt!"

After a ten second section of blank tape, they heard strains of "Malaguena" and suddenly a little boy in a black tux, top hat, and cane was skating. Moe sat smiling as he also went back in time and remembered Victor's performance.

Suzette explained this was one of Ada's first films of Victor in competition. She pointed her finger at Moe. "This is where it all started."

As William and Mary watched the film, they realized they had walked in darkness together with three shadows.